Blitz Bullion Busters II
Cold Gold

Daryl Joyce

Clink
Street

Published by Clink Street Publishing 2023

Copyright © 2023

First edition.

The author asserts the moral right under the Copyright, Designs and Patents Act 1988 to be identified as the author of this work.

ISBNs:
978-1-915785-29-9 Paperback
978-1-915785-30-5 Ebook

To every Year 6 class I've ever taught -
past, present and future.

1

'It's got to be *Wet n Wild* next!' enthused Wade, as he and Jack walked through the amusement park crowds whilst munching into a school-provided sandwich.

'I'd rather go to *Turtle Nugget Crush*,' replied Jack, eyeing his yellow apple suspiciously. He put the ageing apple into his backpack and slung it back over his shoulders smiling.

'We've only got ten minutes before we need to head back – how about that one; the *Terrific Toe Tingler*?'

It was a gloriously warm day and Mrs Poppet's Year Eight class were enjoying Risa Land of Adventures. After all they had been through recently, Jack felt it was great to really begin to relax. What made it better than that, however, was that it was less than two weeks before the glorious six-week summer holidays. Their teachers had allowed them to wander around by themselves with the warning that if there was any trouble, it would be *cleaning the playground with your tongue* time when they got back.

They would have been less relaxed had they known that forty metres away on a seat disguised as a mushroom, a man with a large rucksack sat watching the members of class 8P. *You'll pay* the figure thought as he got up and walked towards Jack and Wade.

'No… no, that!' Wade said suddenly, pointing his crusty sandwich remains at a large Ferris wheel called *Wheel see you soon*. Jack's shoulders fell. The large colourful sign announced that this was the *360° view of your life!*

'Not really keen on heights,' said Jack in a slightly whiny voice. Ignoring him, Wade pulled him to the end of the queue and enthused about what they would see from the top. The queue moved fast and within ten minutes they were at the front.

A man in a hard hat and orange Hi-Viz vest with *Maintenance* written on it suddenly pushed past them and whispered something to the attendant, who nodded sagely and let him past. Keeping his back to them, he bent down in front of the cart closest to them and made some tinkering noises with his tools.

'What's going on?' asked Wade impatiently.

The attendant, whose name badge announced him as *Cecil Bodge*, looked Wade up and down with a smile that seemed too big for his face.

'We just have to check something, sirs. We'll be starting again in just a minute, sirs,' he said through a fixed grin.

'Can you see what he's doing?' whispered Wade to Jack, trying to peer past the man.

'No, but I expect with the thousands of people on this every day, it needs constant minute adjustments and…' replied Jack, his voice trailing off. 'Does he seem—' but before Jack had a chance to finish his sentence, the maintenance man stood up, nodded at the ride attendant, and headed away.

'Whatever – let's go!' said Wade jumping into the cart as Jack followed reluctantly. To him it felt rickety, and he frowned at the thought of being twenty-five metres off the ground in something barely larger than a shopping trolley.

'I don't like these things,' Jack said quietly as it jerked. He grabbed at the bar and kept his eyes forward. Wade, meanwhile, seemed to have no such fears as he leaned this way and that way, pointing at other rides in the park.

'There's *Peeky Penguins* and I've got to go on *'Orrible Obelisk*!' Wade continued to enthuse as Jack worked hard at holding onto the bar and keeping his breathing under control. 'Hey there's our teacher – ooooeeee, Mrs Poppet!' Wade shouted and waved at their teacher who looked to be having a more peaceful time on a bench under a nearby tree. She looked around but, seeing no-one, went back to talking to Mr Ruby. He was the new Computing teacher who had recently started at their school and had reluctantly agreed to go on this last trip of the year.

As they reached the top, the wheel juddered gently and slowed. Jack continued to grip tightly but allowed himself to look a little left and right. Wade didn't notice his friend's panic as he stood up and pointed out *Growling at the Badger Kingdom* at the edge of the park.

'Wade, sit down – we'll fall out!' Jack hissed, gripping even tighter.

'No chance of that, these things are built for safety,' Wade said proudly, banging the side of the cart.

'But we're not,' muttered Jack through clenched teeth. Wade looked at him, shrugged and sat back down with a bump that made Jack grab the bar even tighter.

Just then, the two bolts holding Wade's side sparked and snapped with a sharp clicking sound. The sudden lurching caused the cart to tilt to forty-five degrees and both boys almost fell out.

'What did you do?' shouted Jack accusingly as he pushed with his legs against the side.

'Nothing, I just—' began Wade fearfully as they realised they couldn't stop their slide out of the cart. Wade held on as he watched Jack's bag fall to the ground, landing with a dull thud below at the feet of the growing crowd. The remaining bolt began to bend slowly…

2

Both Jack and Wade shouted and screamed and held on as tightly as they could, but they felt themselves sliding slowly to the lower end of the cart and that twenty-five-metre drop. Wade hooked his elbow around the bar which slowed his slide a little. Jack was pressed against Wade, and it would only be a matter of time.

Below them they could hear screams and shouts. Through his one open eye, Jack could see more people running in their direction amid pointless cries of 'hang on'. There seemed to be a lot of people holding phones up and a few were taking selfies! Slowly they were beginning to lose their grip. After a few long seconds, the bar Jack was holding onto gave a groaning noise and bent causing Jack to scream and slide past Wade. Wade reached out and grabbed frantically at Jack's jacket. There were louder screams and gasps from below.

Jack's sudden descent was stopped, but there was now nothing between his dangling feet and the wheel mechanism below. Jack held his breath and closed his eyes tighter, desperately trying not to move. The cart continued to make creaking noises amidst the sound of the crowd and machinery struggling.

'Don't move, I'm hanging on,' hissed Wade. Jack looked

up with a mixture of appreciation and fear at Wade, who grimaced with the effort. *How much longer can I hold on?* thought Wade as he felt the strength in his fingers begin to lessen.

Suddenly a voice in Wade's ear: 'It's alright, I've got you.' Wade looked over his shoulder and felt someone in mid-air grasp him. *No, not in mid-air, but actually on a long ladder, attached to... attached to a fire engine!* On another ladder, a similar firefighter grabbed Jack and held onto him tightly as they descended slowly.

'Thank you, thank you,' whispered Jack, eyes still tightly shut. They reached the ground to cheers and applause. When he felt ground beneath his feet, Jack opened his eyes and fell to his knees, stopping short of kissing the ground as he heard the applause from onlookers. Two paramedics covered them with blankets and escorted them towards the back of an ambulance. Some police and security personnel urged the relieved crowd back and put barriers up as some of the other children and teachers from Year Eight tried to see what was going on.

'You ok?' Wade said to Jack. Jack shrugged.

'Yeah... my hand hurts a bit though. How 'bout you?'

'Yeah! I'm ok... reckon we could do that again?' enthused Wade.

Jack couldn't tell if he was serious or not.

Three separate people in the crowd of cheering onlookers were frowning, however. One of them quietly cursed as he removed his hard hat and orange Hi-Viz vest and dropped something to the ground. Shaking his head, the figure pushed back through the crowd and headed to the exit. The other two frowning people were Mrs Poppet and Mr Ruby.

'It's always you two, isn't it?' she sighed, walking over to Wade and Jack with Mr Ruby.

Once their teacher was convinced the boys were ok, and the medics confirmed it, she messaged the other teachers who gathered the rest of Year Eight. As they sat on the mound, Jack and Wade were met like true heroes who had survived a momentous brush with death!

'Let me see if I can get any more information about what happened,' said Mr Ruby and he walked over to where the operator, Colin Bodge, was talking to police. Jack watched as they seemed to speak in hushed tones accompanied with many hand gestures.

After a few minutes, Mr Ruby came back to the boys smiling and carrying something.

'Here you go, Mr Roble,' he said, handing it over, 'this is yours I think…'

'Hey, that's my bag!' said Jack excitedly taking the bag offered by Mr Ruby. Jack rummaged through it and his smile turned upside down. 'Oh no, my camera's gone!' Wade and Mr Ruby looked on as Jack went through his bag again. 'Some *plum* stole my camera!' he replied sorely. Since their underground escapades seven weeks earlier, anyone acting like an idiot was described as a *plum*. 'What is my dad going to say?'

Just then some reporters appeared and, after speaking with Mrs Poppet, approached Wade and Jack. Wade enthusiastically regaled the tale again of how they had miraculously escaped death and that it was only by his amazing strength and fortitude that they had survived. At least that's the way he told it – a total of seventeen times before they left the park and another eight times on the coach on the way back to school.

3

Some forty-six miles to the south-east, a woman in a red trench coat approached a secure holding room on the first floor of a large imposing building. She was accompanied by two men and ordered one of the men to wait outside. A small device in the wall scanned her eye and the door slid open. In the room was a small metal desk. Chained to it was a seated man dressed in a pale blue prisoner outfit. He did not look up as they entered. The woman undid her coat and sat down. A few moments passed as she eyed him up and down.

'*Three-Seven* here thinks you'll not say a word, but I've bet him that you will, so don't let me down,' she said with an air of authority. The man looked at Agent Three-Seven with a hint of recognition but stayed silent.

'Onto business then, Mr Plum,' Miss Corner began, 'and you're probably wondering why I'm here.' Plum shuffled slightly in his chair. He had been Miss Corner's top agent until just seven weeks earlier when Faiza, Jack and Wade had thwarted his gold-stealing plans.

'As you can imagine, having to see you is not something I care for, but I'm here professionally to give you some exciting news.' She paused, but still nothing from Plum. 'As you know, your previous security status meant

you had to be tried in secret. The committee have delib-
erated, and it took them about – erm – four seconds to
come to a unanimous decision…' She let the words hang
in the air. Plum moved his head to one side slightly and
narrowed his eyes. 'Their decision is that you *are* guilty
of all crimes you were accused of.' It was Corner's turn to
allow herself a slightly smug smile. No-one said anything
and a whole minute passed. 'Nothing to say then?'

Plum suddenly sat forward and the rattle of the chains
broke the silence. 'I'll help you win your wager. I *do* have
something to say,' Plum eventually said with a mirthless
grin. Miss Corner smiled back towards the suited man
by the door, knowing she had won the bet. Plum had not
finished. 'It's all a fit-up. You and those little… *twonks* did
me up like a kipper.'

'Come come now, Mr Plum, who is really responsible
for your incarceration? You threatened people, including
children, you lied and perverted the course of justice, you
attempted to steal, you appropriated agency resources,
you were disloyal to your country and worst of all you
were traitorous to *me*.' She sat back. He stared at her as
though that alone would turn her to ash.

'You did this; *you* did this – I bet you told them to find
me guilty!' Plum was a little more animated now.

'I don't have *that* much influence… but it would be
fair to say that I helped them reach the right decision,'
Miss Corner said with a shrug of her shoulders. 'But you
incriminated yourself, to be honest. We searched – ran-
sacked might be a better word – your apartment and we
found so many items, a lot of which convicted you by
themselves.' She smiled as Plum pulled at his chain.

'I'm a little embarrassed to say, we're stuck on two
things – can you explain what some of these USB keys
have on them?' Miss Corner held out two iridescent USB

fobs. Plum stared at her, then at the fobs, and then back to her.

'Where.... never seen them before,' he replied, looking away.

'Well, I see you're still no use at lying. Thank you for confirming that they *are* yours. We're having a little trouble with the security on them, maybe you can help us with that?' she asked. Plum continued just staring at her. 'Oh well. We'll crack it soon anyway.' She put them away.

Plum pulled at his restraints and the chains strained against the table with a rasping noise. He sat back and eyed her again.

'Miss Corner, my dear Miss Corner,' he said. 'Still in charge? Still alone, *Miss* Corner, still not married, *Miss* Corner?' He looked at her with dead eyes. Miss Corner simply smiled back in similar fashion. It was not a good look for either of them.

'Nice to see being held in a high-security prison has mellowed you,' Miss Corner replied, 'and what a shame it hasn't improved your vocabulary – you speak like a six-year-old. I feel like you're going to call one of us a *stinky poobum* at any moment,' she said as Plum continued to keep his chains taut in a useless show of defiance.

'You think you're clever, eh? You think you've got me and this all sewn up and I'm stuck here with no-one and no way out... You're wrong. You're so wrong, simply wrong!'

'Oh dear, have I made you angry? How am I mistaken then?'

'You don't know what I'm capable of and you don't know what I've got planned!' he shouted. Agent Three-Seven took a step forward as Plum banged his fists on the table. Miss Corner watched him motionlessly.

'Thank you for that. Very eloquent. Well, anyway, I just

came here to tell you that you're guilty and will be in here for a long time.'

'A long time? We'll see about that. I'm still going to get the rest of that gold! It's me and my family's gold.' His voice was quieter now, but there was still menace behind his eyes.

'Yes, well you *will* be here a *long* time and you can forget about ever looking for any gold – mainly because it doesn't exist. The trail has definitely gone cold.'

'Hah – it does exist and I can still get it and I've got friends you know…'

'You don't have friends,' Corner said quietly as Plum carried on.

'…and family and they will make sure I get what I deserve.'

'I think you're already getting what you deserve,' she replied.

'Not yet, but I will… you just watch me.' he said scowling. 'And I have plans, big plans and I have people out there who will help me!' he shouted again.

Miss Corner looked surprised. 'You've got me there – how could you get any plans to the outside world? You're not allowed visitors or phone calls and your mail is checked, so how on earth could you get or receive any messages?' she asked nonchalantly.

Plum opened his mouth to speak, but then closed it again and shook his head. 'Nice try, Miss Corner, nice try,' he said after a few long moments. He sat back and gave that smug look again.

Corner nodded and shrugged her shoulders. She was about to speak, when Three-Seven passed her a mobile phone. She read the screen and then sighed, passing it back to him.

'We're going,' she said urgently.

'Problem, Miss Corner?' drawled Plum.

'Only for you. Now I think our business is concluded. I have a new urgent business appointment,' she said, getting up to leave.

'Oh, and I was enjoying your company so much,' he replied.

'Well I cannot say the same. Can I tell you one final thing, *Plum*?' She emphasised his name, knowing it would annoy him. 'We know. *And* we are prepared for it. Goodbye, Mr Plum, I hope we don't meet again.'

'Keep looking over your shoulder, Miss Corner, because I'm sure we *will*.'

4

Two hours had passed by the time the coach pulled into school. Both their sets of parents were waiting, as were most of the staff and some journalists. Also standing there, next to a long black car, was someone they were familiar with – Miss Corner.

The fourth floor of LPS House was where most of the 'discussion' suites of CO8 were housed. In Suite Four, Faiza sat one side of a large grey table. It hadn't changed since she was there last, just two months ago. The large room was still relatively bare, with a plain colour scheme. The blandness of the walls was interrupted only by a keypad next to the door. Across the other side of the table was a silver laptop stencilled with *CO8-4* and behind that sat a thin, greasy-haired man in a beige tank-top staring at the screen. There was a big *4* above the door and the keypad now had a hand-guard around it, making it much harder to see a number typed in. Faiza shuffled impatiently in her chair.

'Where the hell are my brother and his sidekick?' she asked suddenly.

'I'm not authorised to answer any questions,' the man said blandly. He peered over the top of his thin glasses and continued to tap on the keyboard. Just then the door opened and in came Jack and Wade. They were accompanied by a tall woman dressed in black trousers and a white shirt. She plonked the two in a chair each and turned and left without a word.

'Where the hell have you been? What's all this about?' she hissed. Wade was about to answer when the tank-topped man spoke.

'Erm, you're not allowed to talk unless an authorised agent is in the room,' he said, turning back to his computer screen. There was a sharp intake of breath as Faiza raised her eyebrows and stood up indignantly.

'I've been rudely picked up on the way home from school without an explanation and I've been sitting here for half an hour now and unless you talk to us now, me and Laurel and Hardy here are leaving.'

'I'm only authorised to tell you that someone will be here shortly.' The man had a look on his face; determined boredom was the best way to describe it. A few silent seconds passed.

'Come on, guys, let's get out of here.' Faiza turned and began to walk towards the door. Just then Miss Corner entered carrying some files and shadowed by one of her operatives.

'You're going nowhere right now, Miss Saab. All of you sit back down, please.' Although she had asked them politely, there was a steely tone to Miss Corner's voice that made Faiza stop on her next step. The boys sat back down, with Faiza reluctantly following suit. Miss Corner sat down and put her files on the table.

'Right, that's better. Now, apologies for the delay, I like to have all the details before I start any *discussion*.' She smiled, but the way she said *discussion* made Jack shiver a little. 'Mr Dank?' She looked over at the man in the beige tank-top, who got up looking a little worried. Wade snorted at the man's name.

'Your laptop's fixed, Miss Corner, and it's all connected correctly now – it was an IP conflict. Sorry about the delay.' He bowed his head and headed rapidly to the door, knocking Miss Corner's files on the floor.

Wade was closest and first to leap up. He helped pick them up, putting them carefully on the desk. Corner stared at a frightened looking Dank, who muttered some apologies and quickly backed towards the door. Shielding the keypad, he typed in what sounded like a six-digit code and, as the door opened, slipped out.

'Computery people,' she muttered.

'What is all that?' asked Wade, shuffling in his seat.

'Just some more Blitz bullion stuff we gathered from Plum's apartment,' she said, as she turned to face the three. 'Now I guess you'd like to know why you're here?'

'Well, that would be a start,' said Faiza frustratedly. She was about to add more when Miss Corner clarified:

'Firstly, it's good to see you all and again, I'm glad you're both ok.' She looked at Wade and Jack. 'That was quite an adventure you had today,' she added. Faiza looked at them confused, but Miss Corner continued. 'I've brought you here to say that we are keeping an eye on things and, after what happened today, we want you to stay safe.' She let the words sink in for a moment. Jack and Wade looked a bit nonplussed. Corner was about to continue when Faiza cut in.

'Someone better tell me what happened!' she said, turning angrily to the two boys.

Wade took a deep breath and detailed everything that had happened earlier that afternoon. As usual, Jack was able to clarify some of the more florid parts of his retelling.

Faiza turned back to face Miss Corner. 'Right, thank you. So why have we ended up here then? Is there something dodgy happening?'

'I have to ask – did you see or hear anything unusual before the ride?' asked Miss Corner

'No,' said Wade quickly. Jack looked at Wade and raised his hand slowly. Miss Corner rolled her eyes before indicating he should speak up.

'Erm,' he began, 'actually, there was that mechanic who came and fixed the ride just before we got on. I don't know what he did, but we were the ones who got on next. And my camera was nicked out of my bag.' Miss Corner nodded and pressed a button on the small control panel.

'Miss Place? Get today's CCTV from the Risa Land of Adventures' *Wheel See You Soon* ride.' She clicked off.

'What's going on, Miss Corner?' asked Faiza growing increasingly inpatient.

Corner paused for a moment as if deciding how to say something. She held her hands up. 'We can't be sure. All I can tell you is that we have reason to believe there may be more going on here than a dodgy fairground ride and a stolen camera.'

'You're talking but not saying much – just what is going on?' Faiza demanded again.

'We're not sure, as I said,' Corner admitted. 'But I want you to know we're working to keep you safe.'

'How are you keeping us safe? It doesn't seem like it,' said Wade pointedly. 'Is it Plum – has he escaped?'

'No, don't worry – he's going to find it almost impossible to get out of his incarceration,' replied Miss Corner.

'*Almost*? So, *are* we in danger then or are we safe?' Jack piped up, feeling a little braver.

Ignoring his question, Miss Corner continued, 'Look, just do normal things in a normal way and don't do anything unsafe and you'll be fine.' There was silence for a few seconds. 'Tell your parents downstairs that all is well, and now, if there's nothing else, I'll get you all a ride back to your homes.'

'Actually, I have an important vital question,' said Wade looking around.

Miss Corner indicated for him to go ahead.

'You only ever show us Suite Four – what's in the other ones?' he asked.

Miss Corner rolled her eyes.

5

'Blimey, I can still hear her voice!' exclaimed Wade as they reached his front door. Faiza stood on the pavement talking to their parents.

'Miss Corner's voice or your sister's?' Jack said quietly. 'Miss Corner wasn't very happy, was she?'

'Yeah… and hey, sorry your camera got nicked,' said Wade heading inside and up the stairs. 'Did you have much on it?'

'I liked that camera…. it still had pics of some of those Underground tours I've been on, and I hadn't uploaded some of them,' he replied glumly. Jack had recently been on the *Hidden Underground* tours – there were many areas of the Underground that were disused or abandoned, something they now had personal experience of. 'I went on loads of them – Charing Cross, Aldgate, even Shepherds Bush. You should try it!'

'Yeah, I hoped maybe you could work out where Plum had stashed the rest of that gold,' Wade moaned.

'We'll work it out one day. You know, what we need is some new information or to get a breakthrough on the old stuff,' replied Jack sitting in front of the desk and turning the computer on. Wade sat on his bed and kicked his shoes off. Thanks to a timely intervention from the

Head of CO8, Wade had recently moved into a three-bed-roomed house which was a definite upgrade on where they used to live. He now had more room to create more mess, according to his dad. The computer screen flickered on.

'So, go on then, *Inspector*, where have we got to?' asked Wade.

Jack sighed and emptied his bag out onto the floor. He picked up a blue folder with *Evidence* written across it. Opening it, he scanned down one of the pages.

'Well, *Chief*, we know that *Horatio Plum* stole five hundred bars of gold in the war and hid them. We managed to find three hundred and eleven of them welded to the underneath of the stairs in the Monument.' They both smiled, recalling how all three of them – Wade, Jack and Faiza – had gone through dangers and excitement looking for the missing gold whilst stopping Mr Blue, a descendant of *Plum*. They called him Mr Blue because of a fondness for unfashionable blue suits. 'We also know that *Plum* was killed during the Blitz a week later.' They sat there looking dejected – every time they talked about it, the trail for the rest of the gold went cold. Jack absent-mindedly clicked on a video file on the desktop and smiled.

For a fortnight after they had found the missing gold, they were the hottest thing around. The video file was Wade's personal favourite and they played it often; it was when all three of them were interviewed on *Lorraine*. Jack and Wade smiled as they recalled those days with inter-view after interview at all the major broadcasters' studios.

'Oh it's really really good to have you heroes here,' Lorraine was saying to the three as they sat in front of her. Only Jack looked uncomfortable. 'So you three wee heroes are amazing and you solved the mystery of the missing gold, it's really, really good. How did you do it?'

'Well, we all worked as a team, led mostly by me,' answered Wade enthusiastically.

'I think we all played a major part in it,' cut in Faiza, elbowing Wade.

'That's really really good.. and you, Jack, are you the brains of the outfit?' Lorraine asked a wide-eyed Jack. He sat there and just shook his head quietly.

'So, Faiza, where did you get those lovely shoes, they're really really good.'

Jack sighed and closed the video. It seemed like a long time ago. Wade smiled and was about to ask Jack to play it again when the door swung open.

'Alright, losers, what's happening in losertown?' Faiza said as she strolled in and sat on Wade's bed, pushing Wade's feet away. He had never found it easy getting on with his 'new' sister, but recently they had got on much better. It helped that he now had the same size bedroom as Faiza.

'So, you two have had quite a day then?' she said nonchalantly.

They both nodded.

'Do you think we're safe?' asked Jack quietly.

'Corner said so much without saying anything and that was frustrating. I think we'll be ok as long as we just keep out of trouble,' replied Faiza reassuringly. 'At least there's nothing dangerous on the horizon.'

'And there we were just wondering whether we would ever find that missing fortune in gold,' sighed Wade.

Jack nodded.

'Haven't you and *Captain Quiet* worked it out yet? Come on, what's the point of having a geeky younger brother when he can't even do my homework?'

'Well, what have *you* come up with?' Wade protested.

'My friend Janet thinks that he chucked it in the river and—' she began.

'He just chucked it in the river? He just *chucked* it in the river,' he mimicked, 'a million quid in gold and hey, I know, let's throw it overboard. She's a genius, that Janet,' Wade announced sarcastically.

'Still a better idea than yours, 'cos you and the *silent scientist* haven't got one!' she replied with a smug face.

'This may help.' Wade looked a little sheepish as he pulled something from his pocket and held his closed hand out to Jack. Jack looked a little puzzled until Wade opened his closed fist. There in his palm was a small shiny object – an iridescent USB fob.

'What is that and… where did you get it?' asked Jack.

'It fell out of that file when the computer bloke knocked it – I just put it in my pocket. Thought it might help us find out more about Plum,' said Wade in a happy tone.

The other two were open-mouthed.

'You did what?! You stole some data from the Head of CO8?!' replied Faiza incredulously.

'She'll crucify us. She'll have our guts for garters!' added Jack.

'I know and I'll… what does that actually mean?' asked Wade.

'I don't know. My dad says it a lot… anyway when she finds out, we're dead meat,' answered Jack, turning the USB key over in his hands.

'I can't believe you just nicked that! I mean it's kind of impressive in a way, but you heard what she said about keeping safe… and Jack's right – she'll lock us up in some dungeon somewhere forever,' said Faiza.

'Well with any luck she'll think it was that computer bloke,' replied Wade a little deflated.

'Maybe we should,' said Jack, 'just give it back?'

'Let's have a look at it first though,' cut in Wade, grabbing the USB key back and sticking it in the computer slot. It didn't go in. He smiled, turned it over and put it in the slot the right way up.

'Hang on, you berk – that could have a virus on it or anything!' hissed Jack incredulously.

'Soon find out!' He grinned.

They looked at the computer that just seemed to be sitting there making the usual quiet humming noises. The hard drive started chuntering with its access light flashing, but it soon settled down. The screen suddenly flickered off. They held their breath briefly as it burst back into life.

'Don't worry, it's always doing that,' said Wade, breathing a mental sigh of relief.

As the file explorer came up, Wade scrolled down to the new drive and double-clicked its name: *Grandad*.

'Grandad? Wow this really must be Plum's,' Faiza whispered to herself. After a few seconds it launched, and a grey box appeared on screen: *Password*.

Both Wade and Faiza looked at Jack who looked equally perplexed.

'How should I know?' he shrugged his shoulders. 'Try a name… how about *Plum*?'

Wade typed it in and after a few seconds it responded with, *Access denied. 9 attempts left. Data will be permanently erased on 10th incorrect password*. They both looked again at Jack, who after a few moments said;

'Hmm, we've only got nine tries left, so we'll need to think carefully.'

'Well, that's Wade out then,' quipped Faiza. Wade just made a sneer.

'How about in capitals?' Wade replied and, before they could stop him, typed the same name in uppercase and pressed enter. Seconds passed.

Access denied. 8 attempts left. Data will be permanently erased on 10th incorrect password'.

'Listen,' said Jack with urgency, 'don't do any more, let's think it over – maybe get some more expert advice…?'

'Who from?' Wade and Faiza asked in unison.

6

'Hello, lads, you're keen,' said Mr Ruby at 8.15 as the boys entered the Computing Suite the next day. Dressed in a smart suit, he didn't seem to quite fit in – you could tell he was a supply teacher. He had replaced Miss Perumal who had happily won the lottery three weeks earlier and never came back.

'Got a problem, sir,' said Wade apologetically, holding out the USB fob. 'I've got loads of my homework on this and I can't remember the password to open it.'

'Right, so presumably you've tried all the usual passwords and the like?' Mr Ruby took the offered memory stick and rolled it over in his hands.

'Yeah done that. The problem is that it's only going to give me eight attempts before erasing. I set the security but now I can't remember the password and I've no idea how to turn it off,' replied Wade sheepishly. Mr Ruby seemed more interested now.

'That's some strong high-level encryption – where did you get it?'

'My sister gave it to me – it just came with the encryption installed,' replied Wade as Mr Ruby continued to turn it over in his hands.

'Well, what I'd suggest is think about what kind of

documents or homework might be on it – say a project or something you may have been working on, and try a common word associated with that. So, if it was about the war, you might try Blitz or Bullion.' He winked at the boys.

'Ok, sir, we'll try that then,' said Wade as Jack held his hand out. Mr Ruby seemed a little reluctant to hand it back to a grateful Jack, who quickly pocketed it.

'Sorry if it's not that helpful but hey, you could always leave it with me. I've got a busy morning in a phase leader meeting and teaching the Year Tens, but after that I could get right on it?' He smiled that disarming smile and the boys looked at each other before shaking their heads.

'No, it's ok, Mr Ruby, you've been very helpful.'

'Well, if you're sure? Let me know how you get on and what you come up with,' he replied.

Thanking him again, they both backed out and headed for the playground.

'Do you think we'll be able to crack it?' asked Wade out of earshot.

'Yeah… I'm not sure who just helped who. I just hope we've done the right thing,' replied Jack mysteriously.

They bumped into Mr Ruby twice more that same day – in the corridor and in the lunch queue. Both times he smiled a lot and asked them how they were getting on deciphering their mysterious password. They just had to explain they hadn't tried yet and would look at it that evening. As Mrs Poppet dismissed the class for the day, Jack looked out of the window.

'That's odd,' whispered Jack as they lined up. 'Mr Ruby is by the gate – you don't think he's waiting for us?' Wade screwed his face up and peered out to where Jack was looking.

'Ugh, I hope not – he's way too keen on that memory stick.'

'Let's avoid him and go out the back way, with the Year Elevens.'

Half an hour later and the three of them sat in Wade's room. As Mr Ruby had done, Faiza turned the shiny USB key over and over in her hands as though that action alone would encourage it to give up its secrets.

'Ruby said it could be a password that is linked to what is on it,' said Jack.

'But we don't know what's on it,' replied Faiza in exasperation.

'No...' replied Jack, 'but Mr Ruby mentioned something to do with gold and the war as an example – don't you find that odd?'

'Nah not really... guess he's heard about what we got up to a few months ago. They do still talk about it a lot in school,' said Wade trying to get the shiny object from Faiza.

'Maybe... but it's quite a specific example,' Jack mused.

'Well, if it was something to do with the missing gold, what could the password be?' said Faiza, trying to move them on.

'Anything – there's probably about two million combinations.'

'Ugh, it's impossible. You think those boffins at CO8 had trouble with it too?' asked Wade.

'If we did, they did! Maybe we'll be the first ones!' said Faiza.

'Right, well presuming it is to do with the gold, and it's a Plum family secret, let's start by writing down all the words it could be,' said Jack, now fired with enthusiasm. The other two looked at each other and grabbed a pen.

7

Over the next twenty minutes through chit-chat and questions, they created a list of thirty-two words they felt were important to the gold find.

'Look, we've got all these words and we can only have the best eight?' moaned Wade.

Jack nodded. Another twenty minutes passed as they discussed the twenty-four they had to drop. Words like *thief, underground, secret, hidden, Greengage, code* and *Damson* were all too obvious or too obscure so had to be dropped.

'What about *Wade*? Or even your name?' said Faiza listlessly, looking at Jack.

'No, I think it's bigger than just us which is why *CO8* probably couldn't open it either,' replied Wade thoughtfully. Other words dropped from the list included *London, railway, King William* and *Horatio.*

All three of them sat in front of Wade's computer with a final list of eight potential passwords. After the usual tedious startup checks, the familiar desktop background of the trio standing with their headteacher holding a fake gold bar appeared – the public recognition of their recent success in finding most of the gold bullion secreted away by Horatio Plum during World War Two.

'Right, we're all agreed – these eight words are the ones most likely to open it IF this memory key is anything to do with Corner and the missing gold,' said Wade.

They nodded, still slightly unsure.

'Let your friend do it – he's good on the computer,' Faiza said.

Wade was about to object, but let Jack have the keyboard. He picked up the memory stick and tried to plug it into the USB port, then he pulled it back and inserted it the right way up. The screen went white and a small box appeared in the middle asking for the password. Jack looked at the other two briefly, before carefully typing in their first word. He said each letter as he did it: 'B-u-l-l-i-o-n.'

Jack paused and pressed enter and a long second later, the screen responded with, *Access denied. 7 attempts left. Data will be permanently erased on 10th incorrect password.*

'Ugh,' Wade whispered. 'Ok, try *Blitz*!'

Jack typed it in, but the screen responded in similar fashion except they now only had six attempts left. The same happened for *gold, Corner* and *Mr Blue* to their increasing despondency.

'It looks like quite a big box to type in – try that *Horatio Plum* one,' said Faiza with more certainty. Jack typed it in carefully. The computer eventually came back with, *Access denied. 2 attempts left. Data will be permanently erased on 10th incorrect password.*

'Oh man, we've only got two chances left,' said Wade less happily.

The screen flickered and went black suddenly. Wade banged it on the side causing it to go black and white before displaying the password box.

'Damn this screen,' Wade muttered. 'I might have to send it back.'

'No, do it again – bang the screen and watch the bottom right-hand corner,' Jack said urgently.

Both Wade and Faiza looked at him strangely, but Wade obliged. They watched intently as the screen flickered black and white before returning to normal.

'Did you see it?' Jack asked.

'What was it?' Faiza and Wade asked in unison. As Wade banged it again, they craned forward to see what looked like a tiny semi-transparent question mark.

'That's a hint!' Jack exclaimed and moved his cursor into the corner which came up with a box. In tiny writing, came the words: *Hint: Lines meet terribly*. It disappeared after five seconds as the screen returned to normal.

'What the *plum* does that mean?' asked Faiza exasperatedly. They looked at the words they had left, *Monument* and *London Bridge*.

Jack thought for a moment.

'Lines could mean the Underground lines and they all meet at London Bridge which is where we had so much fun last time?' said Wade excitedly.

'Go on; type in *London Bridge*,' added Faiza.

'I'm not sure – why would that be terrible for the lines to meet there?' said Jack as Faiza dropped her shoulders.

'Ugh, he always has to spoil things, doesn't he?' said Faiza smirking.

'No – that's just sensible… but I still think it's London Bridge. It could be the lines met there and that's where it all went wrong for Corner,' replied Wade. 'Go on, put it in.'

'Still don't think it's quite right, but whatever.' Jack shook his head and typed it in: 'L-o-n-d-o-n B-r-i-d-g-e.'

The computer seemed to spend even longer thinking about it before replying with, *Access denied. 1 attempt left. Data will be permanently erased after next incorrect password.*

'Hmm, I hope that wasn't you looking smug, *Captain Quiet*,' said Faiza.

'It's hard not to be,' replied Jack, allowing himself a small smile.

'Oh man!' Wade was exasperated. 'What else can it be? C'mon, Jack, keep thinking.'

'Hang on… hang on, you said Corner and the missing gold earlier,' said Jack.

'Yes I remember, but we tried *Corner* and *gold*, didn't we?'

'But look, a corner is where lines meet,' said Jack with some obviousness. The other two nodded slowly as if a lightbulb had come on.

'And the *lines terribly* means?' asked Faiza. Jack stretched his fingers and carefully typed into the waiting box:

'C-o-r-n-e-r-s C-a-l-a-m-i-t-y.' The screen went blank for a moment before a small box appeared on the screen: *Access Granted*.

8

'Wow! Jack you did it!' Wade slapped Jack on the back.

'I always knew you were geeky, but that's amazed even me!' exclaimed Faiza. 'How the hell did you know it was Corner's Calamity?' Jack was about to explain when Wade cut in.

'It's what the whole thing used to be called. Inspector Corner couldn't find the thieves or gold and so it was his calamity.'

'Yeah, brainbox, I remember that bit, I was there – but how did you know, *Jack*, that it was the password?' She looked directly at Jack, who looked a little uncomfortable.

'Well, lines meet at a corner and a terrible thing is a calamity. Kind of simple really.' He tried not to sound smug. Faiza looked at him for a few more seconds and then nodded.

'Ok, I guess you can justifiably look smug for a little while then. That's quite impressive.'

'What's on it then? Does it say where the gold is?' Wade pleaded but he already knew what the answer would be.

Jack just smiled and clicked on the icon of the memory stick. After a short delay, the file explorer launched and displayed were two folders. They stood riveted as Jack clicked on the first folder, titled *Archive*.

It opened after a few seconds. The screen showed several images and documents – most of them titled with some variation of *HPFam*. He opened the first file – *HPFam01*. It was a grainy grey picture of a man and a woman outside an Underground station, but most of the roundel was obscured behind a Routemaster bus and a van – all they could see was *ng*.

They gasped collectively as they recognised the man as *Sir Horatio Plum* – the man who had masterminded the stolen gold plan. They didn't recognise the woman, but both people in the photograph were smiling and holding up their right hand, making a circle with thumb and forefinger. With Wade's magnifying glass, Jack could see that the man was wearing a ring with the increasingly familiar backwards C motif.

'Holy cow – is that old Plum?' asked Faiza.

Jack nodded. 'I've never seen that picture – where was it taken?'

As part of their original 'investigation' they had waded through many pictures and documents to do with the missing gold, but these seemed to be new ones.

'No idea – hey who is that woman?' replied Wade puzzled.

'And which tube station is that?' cut in Faiza, looking closely at the *ng*.

'Ding Dong?' said Wade to no-one else. Faiza just tutted.

'That well-known tube station on the made-up line: *Ding Dong station*?' she quipped.

Jack laughed and zoomed into the picture.

'Not sure where it's taken – some Underground station – and no idea who that woman is. Yet.' Jack smiled weakly. He got his phone out and began taking screenshots of the documents on the screen.

'Just in case we lose the USB,' said Jack matter-of-factly. Faiza rolled her eyes.

'So, you think the USB will do what? Self-destruct in five seconds?' she laughed.

Jack didn't say anything but kept taking copies of all the documents and pictures. Both Wade and Faiza subconsciously moved a few centimetres further away from the screen.

'What's that one?' Wade asked, pointing at the screen. Jack zoomed into a picture of a circular disc. Made of brass, it had a centre dial with *Yale* across it and the numbers one to twelve around the outside. Next to it was a tiny piece of paper with the words *Eight Fifty-Five*.

'Guess there must be something secure in there? What else have we got?' There were a few more files on the USB, mostly just old newspaper front pages and pictures of the Thames. None gave any clue as to where the picture of the man and woman had been taken. Jack zoomed into the next document and peered intently at it.

'This is interesting,' mused Jack.

The screen showed a scribbled note with a single unpunctuated sentence; *go right twice stop at a turn left once past a stop at b turn right stop at c.*

'Well what does that mean?!' said an exasperated Wade. 'Is it directions to the gold? Where do we start?'

'Yeah – go right twice from where? How many steps?' added Faiza. 'Doesn't make sense.'

'Yet,' said Jack quietly. 'Worth bearing in mind though – a lot of this stuff doesn't make sense at the moment. Let's hope we can work it out.'

'Can we do anything with these documents?' said Faiza to no-one after they had been through all the folders on the USB drive. 'Go back to that scribble of the teardrop again.'

Jack did as he was asked and scrolled back through the pictures.

'I wondered about that,' said Jack slowly, 'but what is it?' On the screen was a scanned-in picture of a page from a notebook that at some point had been ripped out and screwed up. On the page was a crudely drawn pencil drawing of an upside-down teardrop. The ends almost joined to complete the image, but not quite.

There were small arrows at the bottom left pointing upwards and a small x about a third of the way along, next to the letters CC *NL 09 126S*.

'It's one of those again, isn't it?' said Faiza rolling her eyes and recalling the cryptic clues that had plagued their last hunt for the missing gold.

Jack and Wade nodded wondering what the code meant this time.

'It's interesting that the pencil drawing looks like that couple's hand gesture,' remarked Jack, drawing the teardrop in the air, 'but I don't know what the code refers to.'

'Well, if you don't know, we sure as hell don't!' laughed Faiza.

Wade looked a little crestfallen but put his arm around Jack.

'I'm sure *we* can work it out together soon, eh, Jack?' replied Wade.

Jack tried to smile. 'Actually, there are so many mysteries here and it gives us more questions than we started with,' he replied, frowning.

'Yay for Captain Positive!' snipped Faiza.

'Like what questions?' asked Wade glaring at Faiza.

'Well, right now, the first question we ought to ask is should we be carrying on with this after Miss Corner's warnings…?'

The other two stopped for a second and appeared to

be pondering Jack's wise words. Wade broke the silence. 'But the gold! It's so close,' he said. 'Come on, let's look at another one!' All three of them moved closer to the screen. 'That one!' Wade grabbed the mouse, scrolled back to a document named *HPFam7* and double-clicked on it. The text editor launched, and it displayed a page of scanned-in handwriting.

Titled *Monument*, it contained lots of facts and figures about the two-hundred-and-two-foot Monument where they had previously found most of the gold. It also showed lots of words and doodles in the margins. In the main text about the Monument, some phrases like *311 steps* and *Golden Orb* were circled. It was the words at the bottom that caught Jack's eye. Underlined were *345* and *Hooke!* Quickly, Jack launched the browser and typed in Hooke and Monument.

'What's going on – what have you found?' asked Faiza as a page of results loaded. No-one answered, but Jack was smiling.

9

10:17 the next morning and all three of them sat on a bench in the July sunshine looking up at the Monument. There was a queue of around twenty people all waiting to get in and the sun reflected madly off the top orb. Faiza kissed her teeth. 'Why have I given up a Saturday morning in bed to be here with you two jokers?'

'It's a tough habit to break,' Wade laughed. 'Another weekend, another trip up the Monument. Wow, I came down those stairs fast.' He recalled how he had hurtled down the stairs in pursuit of Mr Blue and both had come to a sudden stop at the bottom. They had crashed into each other and Mr Blue got his head stuck in the railings. Wade had looked up and seen where *Plum* had hidden the gold. He brought his mind back to the present. 'But really, Jack, why are we here again?'

Jack looked around, thinking of the last time they were here and got ambushed by Mr Blue's henchmen. Today, thankfully, there were just tourists.

'Well, we all know about how we found most of Plum's gold stash under the Monument stairs, but did anyone think that maybe the rest of it might be below ground?' They both looked at him incredulously as he got out the piece of paper he had printed. 'No really, look at those few words scribbled – *Hooke* and *345*. I looked it up properly when I got home – one of the architects – Hooke – built a small lab below the whole thing!'

'Let me get this right. You reckon that there is a secret lab built into the Monument? asked Faiza disbelievingly. 'And in the almost hundred and fifty years since, no-one else has found it?'

'Sounds like a great idea,' cut in Wade, patting Jack on the back.

'Thanks, it's not widely known – never been opened to the public. It was hard to find any details about it. This Hooke bloke built it as a science lab to build a massive telescope,' replied Jack.

Wade and Faiza both gave him a *You've gone mad* look. Suddenly Wade became animated. 'Hang on, you think the rest of the gold is down there?'

Even Faiza stopped. Could it be true? Could the rest of Plum's stolen gold be right under where they had found the first lot?

'Well yes, possibly.' Jack seemed surprised that this was odd to them. 'Apparently, there was a secret entrance at ground level and that leads down to it.' He looked at their disbelieving faces. Wade spoke first.

'So, *Colonel Geek*, how the hell are we going to get down there without anyone noticing?'

Jack smiled weakly and, after swallowing hard, out-lined his idea.

Around eighty metres behind them, a man with a ruck-sack stood looking intently into a coffee shop window. He wasn't looking at the range of pastries or the fifty-eight different types of coffee they had, instead he was look-ing at the reflection. *Why have you come back here again?* he thought. *More visiting old glories that should be ours. Enjoy your freedom whilst it lasts.* He turned away and pulled out his phone. As the man with a rucksack talked into his phone, he was unaware that someone else inside the coffee shop was also very interested in the Monument.

After lining up at the Monument for a few minutes, Wade, Faiza and Jack got to the front and asked for three child tickets.

'Eight pounds ten pence please, young man,' the man said with a bored monotone voice. The three looked at each other and, after a few moments of arguing over who should pay, Jack sighed and angrily pretended to look for money in his rucksack. He pulled out several things whilst mumbling to himself – a sandwich box, a mangled model metal Spitfire, a pack of orange paperclips, a compass, and his phone. After a minute, the queue behind them began to murmur and there were tuts and sounds of teeth kissing. The man behind the booth asked them to move to one side. Still bickering, they moved round to just behind the ticket booth as Jack put the items back in.

Looking up briefly, they noticed that they were being ignored now as the man behind the booth continued to serve the sizeable queue. Jack pointed to a small cream-coloured wooden door, at floor level behind a metal cabinet. They moved further round out of sight.

'That? That small door leads to the gold?' asked Wade excitedly.

'Calm down, it's probably just a cupboard or some pokey door to nowhere,' whispered Faiza.

Jack pulled out the small battle-damaged metal Spitfire and smiled. Wade smiled back; eyes wide – he remembered how they had used the model Spitfire several times before.

'It's like your sonic screwdriver' laughed Wade.

'A what?' Faiza shook her head, not getting the reference to Dr Who's get-out-of-any-troublesome-situation device. 'Just get it open, *Captain Quiet*,' she hissed. Jack prised open the small wooden door. The light flooded a small room behind the door. In it were some buckets and mops.

'Ha, told you it was a cupboard!' laughed Faiza trying hard to keep her voice down.

'That's it? A store cupboard?! Where's the gold?' Wade was clearly unhappy. Jack looked a little bemused and Faiza just rolled her eyes. 'That can't be right – let me check!' Pushing past Jack, he lifted the mop and edged the buckets to one side and spotted a circular wooden base.

'There... look, Wadey – look at that,' Jack said pointing to something crudely carved into the wooden circle. Wade ran his hands over it – there was no doubt; it was a backwards C. Wade smiled and held his hand out to Jack, who nodded and wordlessly handed him the slightly mangled model Spitfire.

Easing a wing edge into the gap between the wood and the concrete floor, Wade struggled to raise the wooden circle. Jack eased into the small room as Faiza kept an eye out behind them. Although they were behind the small metal cabinet, you never knew if someone would hear them or come searching. A small gust of stale air signalled that Wade had managed to prise open the wooden base. It was heavy and clearly hadn't been moved for some time. Wade edged his fingers under it and lifted it. A big spring-loaded hinge on one side stopped it opening more than thirty centimetres. Wade tried but could not lift it any further: the large, rusted spring trying to pull it shut. With a big smile, he put his head to one side on the floor and peered into the darkness.

10

'I can't see anything except some steps,' he whined a few seconds later.

'If only your personality could light up what's down there,' said Faiza edging closer. Jack closed the small door behind them cutting out most of what was left of the light. The only sound they could hear was the distant muffled murmuring from the queue. 'Don't suppose there's a light on that plane thing?' she asked.

Jack shook his head and instead pulled out his phone. He switched on the torch app and angled it through the hole. It lit up the circular walls and the first few steps but little more.

'Oh come on, the gold could be at the bottom of those steps!' Wade eased his feet through the opening.

'Are you sure? Be careful – I don't want to end up telling your dad how you got eaten by a giant rat!' laughed Faiza.

Wade smiled and edged his legs through the gap and found the first step. As he did so, his knee caught Jack's phone, sending it flying.

'Wade!' said Jack exasperatedly. He looked down and watched the light bounce around for a few seconds before a crunch which extinguished the light. Wade looked back up with a sorrowful look on his face;

'Sorry, Jack, I didn't see it and—'

'Always rushing in without a thought, clumsy arse,' said Jack crossly.

Faiza opened her eyes wide and nodded slowly at Jack.

'Hey, Jack, you've got some *garumba* after all! Wade, you *can* be a right arse. Just be careful.'

'Sorry, Jack. Look I didn't mean it, it was an accident,' Wade said sorrowfully.

Jack just shook his head.

'How far down is it?' Jack said quietly after a moment.

'Probably about ten metres, it only took a few seconds for, erm, for the light to go out. I'll go down and get it. Jack, come on – this could be where we find our fortune – you could buy a hundred new phones!'

'It could also be a tunnel of doom or some sewer... again! Well, I'm not going down there!' Faiza was adamant.

'I am! It's a stone staircase – I'll be alright,' said Wade. His face faded and he disappeared into the darkness. The wooden lid lowered with a gust of air as Wade let it go. There was silence.

I'll be alright, he thought to himself. *I'll be alright.* The stone steps were cold and covered in a sticky dust. Wade was sure he could hear noises. *I'll be alright*, he thought again. He couldn't tell whether his eyes were open or not. All about him the air seemed to move slowly. He cocked his head to one side. Was that movement below him? *That's just the air moving*, he thought *maybe some insect or other*. There was a rancid smell. *That's the dead insects and dust... all rotten and old*. Water seemed to be dripping somewhere. *Just what is waiting below me?* Was that the sound of water swirling? *I must be imagining it.* He wouldn't admit it, but he was scared, very scared, and moved very slowly... down, down, into the watery darkness.

Two long minutes passed. Jack lifted the wooden lid and whispered. 'Wade?' No reply. 'Wade?' Still no reply. Jack couldn't hear or see anything. He looked back at Faiza who slowly nodded. He sighed and lifted the wooden lid, hoping he could see or hear something of Wade... but nothing. Even the air seemed to have stopped moving.

Looking up one last time at Faiza, Jack frowned and gulped. He put his bag and mangled Spitfire to the side of the hole. Sighing inwardly, he lay on his front, pushed his feet over the edge and squeezed between the edge of the floor and the wooden lid. Faiza watched him go and, despite the scuffling noises coming from the hole, felt suddenly alone. She looked around in the semi-darkness... The air seemed cooler and there was an eerie feeling about the place.

'Wade?' Jack whispered. There was no reply, just the noises of scuffling (*or was it splashing?*) a few metres below him in the darkness. He was surprised that there was no echo. The wooden lid above his head closed with a light whoosh of air and then he couldn't see anything at all. Carefully, slowly, deliberately, he used his hands and feet to feel his way down the steps. It was like they were in a stone cylinder but *what was that smell*? Below him in the darkness there was a distant scuffling sound which he hoped was Wade... but why wasn't he answering? There was also a distant splashing and dripping sound... how could that be? 'I'll be alright,' he muttered to himself. 'I'll be alright.' Slow step followed slow step, down, down.

Less than two minutes of slow descent later, Jack put his left foot down and gasped as he felt icy water soak through his shoe and sock. He shivered and put his other foot into the water. The water swirled in the darkness and was about twenty centimetres deep. It smelled stagnant.

'What do you think?' said Wade loudly, breaking the silence and splashing towards him in the darkness. Jack jumped.

'Blimey, *Way*. Why didn't you answer?' asked Jack standing up.

Wade shrugged his shoulders. 'Erm, sorry, I got distracted feeling my way around.' But he was laughing as he said it, so Jack knew he'd stayed silent on purpose.

'Well, it wasn't funny.' Jack frowned.

'There is some stuff down here… but it's cold, smelly and wet!' replied Wade ignoring Jack's annoyed tone.

'So are we, now. Right, so what have you found?' replied Jack.

'Not much to see yet but I found this on the bottom step!' said Wade excitedly. Jack jumped again as he felt Wade thrust something at his shoulders. It was his phone. He shook it – it seemed alright, so he flicked the on switch and the screen burst into life, flooding the area with light. The screen was sadly cracked so the light patterns were jagged and cast strange, almost ominous shadows. Jack tutted.

'I said I'd get you a new one,' snapped Wade as they both looked around. Squinting, they could see they were in a circular three-metre diameter stone chamber. Five metres above them they could make out a flat roof with the wooden lid close to the top of the stairs. Water was dripping through a few holes about halfway up the walls. There was slime where the water had dripped down the wall over the years.

Just then Jack jumped and gave a little scream, which also made Wade jump. He grabbed Wade's arm and pushed the light beam round to the other side of the water. A small creature which may have once been a rat was floating on its back. The bobbing of the water made it seem like it was moving. They both stared at it for a few moments, almost daring it to move. It didn't.

'Ugh!' was all either of them could say. The jagged light shone on six or more old empty tins of *Flatlux* white paint half submerged in the water, the shadows creating strange shapes and indents on the walls. As they shone the light further round, they saw more of the 'stuff' that Wade had mentioned – two metal boxes stacked on top of each other. Wade strode purposely through the water over to the boxes and pulled open the lid of the top box. Reaching inside, he pulled out a stiff paintbrush and threw it into the water. The metal box clanked as Wade put it aside and lifted the lid of the second one.

'Jack.. bring the light here.. bring it now!'

11

The light from Jack's phone lit up the inside of the box. Inside were some splashes of white paint and at the bottom, under another ancient paintbrush, were two small white bars. Wade reached in and pulled them out, feeling their weight. His eyes were as wide as his smile.

'It's gold… it's just like the other ones we found!' He spoke very fast, clearly excited. Jack shone the light on the small bars in Wade's hands.

'Wade that's amazing! Wow, we've done it!' Their smiles shone in the semi-darkness, but the euphoria was short-lived.

'There must be more!' cried Wade, lifting empty boxes and letting them drop back into the water.

'I can't see any more. Maybe they just left those here?' volunteered Jack.

'But we've found gold – it must be here!' he repeated. He looked around again, a white bar in each hand. Remembering where they had found the last stash, Wade asked, 'How about the stairs?' But these stairs were different; there was no *underneath* as the staircase was formed from stone.

Wade fell to his knees in the water and began feeling around the floor under the water. He made several faces and his hands moved over the slimy floor, as Jack shone the light onto the now turbulent water. He made sure he went nowhere near the thing that once was a rat. A minute passed and Jack called Wade's name. Reluctantly Wade stood up again. He was dripping and looked dejected.

'It's no use, mate,' said Jack quietly.

Wade was about to protest, but instead closed his mouth and just nodded. 'Damn, I really thought I'd... we'd found the rest of the gold,' he moaned.

'But we did find two whole bars!'

'Yeah... maybe you're right. Hey.' Wade grinned. 'Let's not tell Faiza!'

'I don't think that's a good idea if you want to see your next birthday!' laughed Jack shaking his head.

'I know, I know. I was only kidding,' said Wade. 'I'll hold onto the bars for now.'

'Come on, I think we need to get out of here. My feet are soaking and you're smelling worse every minute,' said Jack heading back towards the bottom step. Wade looked at Jack in the darkness, but before he could speak, Jack did. 'Yes I *am* sure we should tell Faiza, before you ask again,' said Jack.

Wade harrumphed as they got to the base of the stone steps.

Wade held the two white bars aloft as he followed Jack up the stairs – it was a lot easier and quicker with the light from Jack in front. Jack pushed the wooden lid up and crawled out, followed by a slightly bedraggled but smiling Wade, and stood up in the small cupboard, dripping. Despite the darkness in there, they could tell they were on their own. Faiza had vanished.

'Where is she?' asked Wade. Jack shone the light around the small room, but it was empty apart from the buckets and mop from earlier. Wade put the bars into his pocket.

'Bet she got in a mood and went for some hairspray.' Wade went to open the door.

'Hang on, can you hear that?' asked Jack craning his neck.

They listened.

'Nothing, what can you hear?'

'Nothing – that's the point. Shouldn't we hear people going up the stairs or in the queue?'

'Well, maybe they're just quiet. I'm going to go and tell Faiza about OUR gold!'

'Wait a minute, she wouldn't just—' started Jack, but Wade had already opened the door.

The small room was flooded with light and from where Jack was standing Wade seemed to fly soundlessly forward into the light. Jack gasped and tried uselessly to duck behind the bucket, but a large wolf-sized dog came out of the light and barked loudly. He leapt from the room past the loud dog and into the large arms of a gorilla dressed in a black suit.

Jack struggled but it was like fighting treacle and the arms held him fast. In front of him was Wade, also struggling in the vice-like grip of a large, suited gorilla, and there was Faiza standing next to Miss Corner, head of CO8. Faiza's surprise turned quickly to infuriation – she glared at Wade.

'You couldn't have stayed in there another ten seconds, could you?' Faiza hissed. 'I told them I was on my own and I was just leaving.'

Miss Corner meanwhile frowned as her shoulders slumped.

'So it *is* all three of you again, and after what I told you two days ago. Right, don't say another word,' she said in her familiar Northern Irish drawl. Giving a barely notice-able nod, the two operatives holding Wade and Jack released them. The boys straightened up and shook themselves down.

'Miss Corner?' said Wade disbelievingly.

Before she could reply, a large woman and a man with a camera burst through the Monument entrance. The man took several pictures accompanied by an overly bright flash and the woman spoke like a machine gun, 'Bobbi Dudman, *Evening Chronicle* – What's going on? Why are you here? Have you found the remainder of the gold? Are you arresting them? Why are you recruiting teenagers to do your spy work? Can we have a—'

Corner gave another nod to her operatives who effortlessly bulldozed the reporter and her photographer back through the entrance and outside. She breathed out loudly over the noise of Dudman's complaining. 'How did she know about this so quickly? Damn that *Dudman*. Right, this place is too public. Three-Seven and Four-Five? Get them to LPS House – isolation protocol. Suite Four.' She pointed at six operatives dressed all in black and then back to the small room and they rapidly deployed.

As they passed her, she swished out of the Monument. Two large, suited operatives ushered the three out, each into a separate small black van with blacked-out windows.

12

Jack and Wade were ushered into the room – *Discussion Suite Four* of course – and sat down around the familiar long desk. Across from them stood Miss Corner. She peered over her reading glasses at them in silence, just as Faiza was escorted in.

'Maybe we should get you your own parking spot?' In case they weren't aware, her face showed she was not happy.

Wade was about to speak when Faiza cut across him, 'Why are we here again? You could have just taken a photo of us; you didn't need to kidnap us.'

Miss Corner held up a hand. 'I'm asking the questions, Miss Saab. In the meantime, fear not, I've let your parents know that we have you here for a safety debriefing. So yes, we've brought you all back together again just before I either charge you or lock you up downstairs forever.'

There's no way of telling if she's joking or serious, thought Wade.

'To save time and made-up half-truths, let me tell you what we have so far: for some as yet unidentified reason you all decided to head back to the Monument – the scene of your last debacle. And on a whim manage to find an entrance that has been hidden for the best part of a century?' All three of them nodded in agreement. 'Why were you there?'

'We were just out to visit our old haunts – we still love the Monument; it's where it all happened,' replied Faiza indignantly.

'Hmm, I wondered if you got some new information maybe. We all agreed things are… not safe at the moment and you definitely should not go looking for the remainder of that cursed gold.'

The three looked suitably taken aback.

'We wouldn't go looking for any gold!' said Wade plaintively. 'We heard your warnings and, anyway, where would we get new information from? That trail has gone cold!' He held his hands up.

Miss Corner eyed each of them suspiciously.

'Hmm. Let me continue: With Miss Saab hanging around upstairs, you two splash around in a vermin-infested pool, before miraculously finding two bars of the gold. What a piece of coincidental luck. Like to explain why or how?' Miss Corner raised an eyebrow at them. Faiza turned to Wade.

'You found some gold?! And when were you going to tell me? You'd better not have been trying to keep it for yourselves.'

'No way, no way!' protested Wade. He turned to Corner. 'We simply had a look around, found the door and, erm, decided to go for a swim.'

'In the dark. In freezing water. With dead rats?' Miss Corner asked incredulously.

'We got lucky with the gold,' said Wade, 'so I guess Plum must have dropped some there when he hid the first lot and we were going to give it back as soon as we got upstairs and—' Miss Corner held up a hand and Wade's voice rapidly disappeared.

'Right. I don't think I believe your reasons for being there today, but I have no evidence to back my hunch. Whilst I'm impressed at your detective skills, I am also furious that you have put yourselves in danger yet again.' She let the words hang in the air and it seemed to take the wind out of their sails. 'I've told you before, you *cannot* do this – you have made a bad situation ten times worse multiplied by ten times more dangerous. There is danger here.'

Ten times worse multiplied by ten times the danger is a hundred lots of terrible – that's pretty bad, Jack thought.

'Danger from what? A dead rat?' replied an indignant Wade.

'Listen. There are… elements that would stop at nothing to get that gold and they don't care who they stomp on in the process. You are to cease this cowboy detective nonsense.' The three looked a little perplexed. 'Just so you know, we've searched the rest of the area and there is no more gold down there.'

'None?' Wade's shoulders slumped.

'Look, if I find that you're chasing that calamitous, damnable gold, I really will pull you in here and leave you in the deepest, darkest dungeon we have.'

'Told you she'd do that!' whispered Jack.

'And I will, trust me. Now which one of you called the papers – that Miss Dudman of the *Chronicle* got there very fast.'

The three looked at each other, shrugging shoulders.

'None of us would do that,' replied Faiza defensively. 'Hang on, how did *you* know we were there?'

Miss Corner shuffled a little in her seat. 'I'm not talking about me.' She turned to Jack. 'Mr Roble, is all of this true so far?'

Jack felt himself wither a little under her gaze and

swallowed. 'It is, Miss Corner,' he said, 'and I really don't like dangerous stuff and I think we'd like to go home soon... and stay there.'

'Good, good.' Miss Corner nodded slowly. She softened her stance. 'Look, it's nice to see you, but, to be honest and with all due respect, I kind of hoped I wouldn't see you all again. This is serious, and I want you to be safe and careful. No more going on a wild goose hunt.' The three continued to just look at her but said nothing. 'Do you understand?'

'Yes, Miss Corner,' they said in unison.

She looked them up and down for a few moments as though pondering some great decision. Her face gave nothing away. 'So, I'm going to tell you one more time: It is not safe at the moment for reasons I cannot go into. I am ordering you to just go home and watch some TV or go on The *ChattySnap* or *Facecloth*, whatever it is that you young people do. But no gold hunting.' She watched and waited for their reactions before continuing, 'I will know if you do, and you can trust me on that too.'

Before ushering them out, she handed over her card and said to contact her if they felt in danger or if they had any more information to tell her. 'I meant what I said,' she added as they got to the door, 'and if you go gold hunting again, we'll meet in Discussion Suite *Five*.'

13

Half an hour after they had arrived, they were ushered into a blacked-out car and left through the back entrance of LPS House. It seemed odd to them that the sun was still shining, and the city was as busy as ever as they headed over the Thames towards Stockwell.

'Blimey, she was definitely clear about keeping out of it now – and wow: finding that gold must have been amazing!' added Faiza.

'Oh yeah – and we found a dead rat! So what happened to you?'

'There I was minding my own business, when all these vans and people pulled up and I just managed to convince them I had no idea where you were! We were just about to leave when – bam – you came through the door!' she laughed.

'There's something not right about this,' said Jack solemnly. They looked at him. 'I mean why keep warning us off if nothing is going on?'

'Wow, do you think there is more out there?' asked Wade, eyes open wider.

'Ugh, I hope not,' said Jack and Faiza together.

But there is something out there, thought Jack.

The traffic grew heavier as they closed in on Brixton

and Stockwell. Jack gasped and pointed out the window. The others looked to where he was pointing. There was Stockwell station, as busy as ever. Nothing looked amiss. Jack whispered, 'The news.' They looked again at the boards next to where some woman was handing out copies of the *London Chronicle* to anyone that wanted one. One board read, *It's the Goldbusters!* and the other said, *Blitz Bullion Bonanza!* They looked at each other in a mixture of shock and pride.

'Excuse me, Mr agent driver,' said Faiza in a sweeter-than-usual voice. 'Can we get a paper on the way home?'

The driver thought for a second before nodding and pulling over.

On the front page and, true to the board, the headline shouted *Goldbusters Strike Again* with a subheading that declared *More War Loot Recovered*. Next to it was a black and white picture of the three of them looking worried, by the entrance to the Monument, taken just hours earlier. he journalist claiming credit for the story was *Bobbi Dudman*.

Fifteen minutes later and all three walked into Wade's room. Wade looked around... something wasn't right, but he couldn't put his finger on it. It looked tidier – maybe that was it; his parents were always tidying up – *why did adults always find it necessary to spend their life tidying*? Jack got on the computer and Faiza and Wade sat on Wade's bed as Wade read more of the article.

'*Earlier today the three Goldbusting heroes found more of the bullion that went missing in World War Two.*'

'Yeah,' said Faiza dryly, 'we're all heroes. What else is there?'

'She knows we only found one or two bars,' said Wade happily. 'But most of it is a rehash of how we're marvellous and how we found the gold before. We sound great!' replied Wade enthusiastically.

'We are. Hey, pass the paper here,' replied Faiza.

She scanned the article. 'Hey, there's more – *It is unclear why three inexperienced and amateur teenagers have been recruited by the security services to find the gold – possibly due to the ineptitude of their ageing chief, who we are unable to name due to security reasons.*'

'*Ageing chief*! Miss Corner will be livid!' Wade laughed.

Jack turned to Wade, frowning. 'So many inaccuracies and questions – who told Corner we were there and how did Dudman know we were there as well?'

'But Dudman obviously still thinks there's more gold – *The three young heroes were prevented in their recovery of all the remaining gold by members of the security forces. We asked for an interview, but this was declined, again, apparently for security reasons*,' Faiza read.

'Is someone really trying to get us?' asked Wade.

'We're not important enough for anyone to come after us – it's not like we got to keep the gold we found,' replied Faiza.

'But it does feel like someone is stopping us,' Jack added.

'It just doesn't make sense; who would do that?' questioned Wade to no-one.

'And, possibly more importantly, why?' Jack asked, then added, 'Why are people always after us?'

Faiza put the paper down and looked at Wade and Jack. 'Good point. Look – don't get me wrong – I find this as exciting as the next person, but maybe it's over now,' she said quietly.

Jack and Wade looked at each other.

'If it is, it leaves so many unanswered questions,' added Jack quietly.

'It's over?' replied Wade indignantly. 'No way – if there's more out there, it's our duty to go find it.'

'Yeah maybe, but you said that just before we had the

run-in with Mr Blue last time.' Faiza shook her head. 'No, I mean it's good fun and I enjoy all the thrill of the hunt, but it feels too dangerous sometimes. What do you think, *humble Harry*?' She looked at Jack, who thought for a moment.

'Truthfully... It does make me feel anxious sometimes and, exciting and baffling though it is, I wonder whether we shouldn't just leave it till it settles down.' Jack shrugged his shoulders.

Wade shook his head. 'Oh no, come on, let's check all these unanswered questions a bit more – who can leave a mystery just dangling? I don't want to do it by myself... come on, we're the three Blitz Bullion Busters... we can do this!' Wade beamed at Faiza, then Jack.

Jack shrugged his shoulders. 'Yeah... yeah of course, maybe we can just do a bit of research... we work well together. I suppose there are more than a few things we could look at...'

'Hmm maybe, we could always keep looking, especially if there's still a mystery and we can do it together,' said Faiza showing a usually hidden sympathetic side.

'Ahhh, that almost sounded like you care.' Wade beamed, tilting his head to one side sympathetically.

'Ugh, no way – I just don't want to go outside the family if I ever need a new kidney,' she replied.

14

Sunday morning and the sun had already been up for a long time. Across the road from Wade's house sat an old lady on a bench. She had a rucksack next to her and watched as Jack walked up and knocked on the front door. As Faiza opened the front door, Jack took a quick look around before following her in and up the stairs.

Faiza rapped on Wade's bedroom door. 'If you don't get up now, I'm going to show your little friend here that picture of you in a—'

'I'm up, I'm up!' interrupted a weary Wade leaping out of bed and opening his bedroom door. Jack stood there looking amused with Faiza who made a face like she had just eaten cat food.

'Is there a hedge in here that you were dragged backwards through?' she smirked.

'That's rich – remember I've seen your hair before it's set in that blue concrete,' Wade retorted, wrapping his dressing gown tighter. There was an uneasy silence for a few seconds as Jack eased past her and sat in the chair in front of the computer.

'Nice one.' She smiled through mock gritted teeth. 'Look, I was going to go shopping with Janet.'

'And now you're not?' asked Wade.

'Nah, she just cancelled – got an emergency dentist appointment; apparently one of her teeth is sharper than the other,' replied Faiza, shrugging her shoulders.

Wade didn't know quite what to say about that. Eventually he asked, 'What did she want from the shops?'

'Oddly, she wanted to find a left-handed screwdriver – heard about it on social media.' Faiza shrugged her shoulders.

'That sounds amazing. Wow, I hope she finds one,' said Wade. 'Why are you smiling, Jack?'

'No reason… maybe she'll find one next to the glass hammers,' replied Jack laughing. He got up and looked out of the window. All seemed calm. Just then, the old lady on the bench opposite looked up, put on her rucksack, and shuffled away. 'Do you think that old lady is watching us? I noticed her earlier. She doesn't seem quite right.' Jack got out of the way as Wade pushed to the windowsill.

'I can't see anyone, you're imagining it,' he exclaimed, closing the curtains. 'Maybe she's turned into a lamp post or she's got a cloak of invisibility?' It was Wade's turn to laugh.

'It's just that you don't see many old ladies with rucksacks. Maybe you're right, maybe I'm just getting anxious over nothing.'

Around the corner, the 'old lady' got into a car and removed a wig and silicone face mask, muttering, *'Plenty of time, plenty of time. And now you've found more of my gold, I'm really going to make you pay.'* At the same time, a man standing in the doorway shadows took note of the car's number plate and walked back inside the house, closing the door.

Jack switched on the computer. 'Hey, how did it go with your parents after yesterday? I listened to my parents drone on for ages, then they read the papers and that seemed to add to their… unhappiness,' Jack said to Wade.

'Hmm, mine too,' replied Wade recalling the strict instructions not to go looking for trouble. 'Me and Faiza were in a bit of trouble, but I had to promise we wouldn't go looking for anything shiny and daft anymore. They made Faiza promise too.'

'Yeah, they were hard on me especially. They said I had led you into this again and I was obviously not as grown-up as I thought,' sighed Faiza. 'What did your parents say, Jack?'

'Same as yours I expect,' replied Jack frowning, 'they wanted to know exactly what was really going on. I told them most of the truth, but not all of it. They seem to think you're a bad influence, Wade, ha ha!'

'Me? You're the one who leads us both astray!' laughed Wade. 'It could have been a bit of Faiza too. Right, fire up the computer and I'll go and get some breakfast.'

'Good idea,' Faiza added and they headed downstairs. Jack turned and faced the computer which continued to start up. There was the usual whirring, and the screen flashed a few times before settling into its usual login page. It flickered momentarily. As he logged in using Wade's password, it seemed a lot slower than yesterday and the light next to the webcam flickered on and off.

A few minutes later and Wade came back in with a sloppy bowl of cereal, followed by Faiza with a bowl of fruit. Wade looked at Jack who turned to face them with a constipated look on his face. Behind him, Wade's computer sat silently staring back at them. They both looked at Jack in puzzlement.

'Ah,' Jack said suddenly, 'I've got it! I know where some more gold is!'

There were a few seconds of stunned silence as the words sank in.

'Say that again…' said Faiza slowly. Wade was also

slightly nonplussed as Jack seemed to be pointing at himself as he spoke slowly.

'I said, I've worked it out – the line that was on that teardrop sheet said, *South to Stockwell*, well that can't be the route after all, it's where the gold is – under the platform at Stockwell Tube!'

'Ok,' said Wade slowly. And then he twigged. Jack wasn't pointing at himself; he was pointing at the computer behind him. 'So, shall we – erm – go and check it out?'

Faiza stopped mid-munch and frowned. She was about to ask what was going on when Jack spoke.

'We should get going quick – let me just check out the station layout on the computer.' Jack turned round and fired up the browser. With his left hand, he scribbled a message and handed it quietly to Wade. Wade tried to read it without really looking at it; it read, *Being watched. Get out.* He passed it covertly to Faiza who maintained a deadpan face. Meanwhile Jack continued to talk.

'Ok, so if we go in the main entrance here, and head down to the northbound platform that goes to Oval station – remember the other document said it was oval shaped; it's all code – gosh that Plum was a wily one eh.'

'Too right. Let's go then!' said Faiza loudly.

Jack switched off the computer and all three of them headed out of the door, Jack grabbing his coat and Wade's baseball cap. A few seconds later, Wade came back in shouting.

'I'll just get dressed first!'

15

They walked quickly but silently out and along the road. Out of sight of the house, they stopped at the corner.

'What's going on, Jack?' asked Wade, quietly looking around.

'Yes, come on, *Mister Mysterious* – I was in the middle of my breakfast,' continued Faiza.

Jack breathed a long sigh. 'We were being watched, or at least overheard. We were bugged in your room – it's the only explanation!'

'What? But how?' asked Faiza.

'Wade's computer – I think someone came in and bugged it whilst we were out,' replied Jack.

'What? No way, that was... well, how do you know that?' said Wade a little sheepishly.

'The way it started up – that screen flicker means the processor is having to do extra things – in this case, sending data to somewhere else. I think either the mic or camera or both have been activated by some stealth spyware. They also hadn't disabled the webcam activation light, so it was a giveaway.'

'Blimey.'

'Sometimes, I'm glad you're so geeky. Sometimes.'

Faiza smiled. They continued to look around themselves, talking quietly.

'So why are we going to… ah, very clever, my old friend!' said Wade, suddenly realising the message they had just given anyone who was listening. 'For a minute I thought that you were talking nonsense about gold at Stockwell!'

'Glad you got it!' replied Jack a little happier.

'I'll give them a piece of my mind if we do find some-one,' added a determined Faiza.

'Careful, there isn't much to spare,' laughed Wade. Faiza just stared at him. 'Right, so let's go look at Stockwell and see if someone turns up!'

'Would it be wrong to hope no-one shows up?' Jack sighed quietly, walking to catch up.

Eight minutes later and they arrived at Stockwell station. Wade had agreed to go and wait on the southbound plat-form, Faiza on the northbound platform whilst Jack waited by the control room. From where he was, he could see not only the ticket office, but also the CCTV screens. He had reversed his coat and was wearing the cap. Wade was at one end of the platform trying to look as inconspicuous as possible, looking intently at space beneath a bench and pretending to be interested in the posters. Faiza was doing the same as she sat on the metal bench. There were a lot of people coming onto the platform on their way to central London or beyond, but no-one seemed to be paying par-ticular attention to either Faiza or Wade. Even the station attendants in orange vests seemed to barely notice them.

Seconds passed. Minutes passed. Yet more minutes passed, and still no-one seemed to be observing Wade, Faiza or himself. They'd agreed on a fifteen-minute wait before they came back up and it was already twenty min-utes. Wade looked up at the camera and shrugged his shoulders. Jack could see Faiza was also looking bored.

As Wade walked out of shot, a train came into the station. Just as Jack was about to look away from the screen, he thought he spotted a familiar jacket and face. He opened his eyes wide and looked hard at the moving crowd on the grey image and tried to make out whether he had just seen someone he recognised.

A minute later, Wade came up and through the gates to where Jack was.

'No luck then eh?' he said sadly.

Jack was staring intently at the crowd. 'Hang on, keep an eye on those people coming up! See if there's someone you recognise!' he replied quietly but urgently. Just then Faiza came and joined them, exclaiming she hadn't seen anyone either. All three watched the throng of people coming up the stairs trying to see if there was anyone that they knew. Another ten minutes passed as trains and people came and went.

'Nah, no-one,' said Wade with a hint of sadness. 'Who did you think you saw?'

'For a second, for a brief second, I thought I saw Mr Ruby.'

At home, Faiza sat next to Wade on his bed with Jack at the computer again.

'Drat that elusive gold – I still think it's at Stockwell,' mumbled Wade as Jack looked at the layout of the Underground station on the internet.

'Could be, but those pictures we saw; one of them had a diagram and if you look at the escalator layout at Stockwell, it follows the pattern of that diagram,' said Jack jabbing a finger at the screen.

'Hey, you're right – and you know what? When we were there earlier, I thought I might have seen a hidden door at the base of one of them. We should go find it!' enthused Wade.

'Well, that's great, but maybe we should wait till after school tomorrow!' replied Jack.

Wade looked thoughtful before replying, 'Good idea – Dad's asked me to help him clean the barbecue today anyway.'

'I need to get home for lunch too. Will call you later.' Jack logged out of the computer and left, leaving Wade tidying his room and trying not to look at the computer, which seemed to be staring at him.

They had agreed on the way back that if the computer was suspect, they would continue to talk in code in his room or feed completely wrong information in case anyone really was listening. They had to act nonchalantly as though everything was normal. So, a few minutes later, Wade powered down and unplugged the computer. He then spent another half hour looking all around the room for anything out of place. He found nothing and smiled as he headed downstairs and into the garden.

16

'And I switched that computer off and stuck it in my wardrobe – not using that again!' said Wade as they made their way into school early the next day.

'Good idea. Well at least we can use the school internet,' said Jack.

'Are you sure school will be open this early?' Wade looked around himself, still feeling that they were being watched.

'They open up the community entrance after seven for the Year Elevens to do studying – I've used it many times and no-one's ever noticed me,' said Jack, almost with a hint of sadness.

The pair sneaked up the back stairs past the staffroom and into the computer suite. They happily noted it was empty, unsurprising since it was only just past 7:15 AM. They kept the lights off and sat out of view of the door.

'You know *she* did say not to go looking for the gold…' said Jack mournfully.

'Well actually *she* said if she caught us again, then she'd lock us up. What that really means is she has to catch us first,' replied Wade with a grin.

Jack just frowned and logged into the school network

and, from his cloud account, pulled up some of the documents.

'We still don't quite get where that pic is of,' said Wade. He was looking again at the picture of Plum and the unknown woman in front of the unidentified Underground station. There was a bus going past an Underground station with only the letters *ng* visible. Jack pondered it, zooming in and out of it to try and get a better view.

'There can't be many stations with *ng* in, surely!' moaned Wade, trying to get a better look. Jack went back to the search engine and brought up a map of the Underground with a list of stations.

'There's about eight or nine so far – Angel, Charing Cross, Barking... even High Street Kensington,' said Jack a little dispirited.

'Oh brilliant,' said Wade sarcastically. 'So, if there is any more gold, it must be at one of the stations?'

'Maybe, but it would have to be easily accessible and quite close to the Thames. There is a space after the *ng* so that may help. It looks familiar though. When we've got more time, we'll pin down the right station.'

Jack moved onto another newspaper cutting – it reported on Sir Horatio Plum getting killed in the Blitz on Hungerford Bridge on 9th September 1940.

'Now we know where he was!' said Wade proudly. 'But where was he coming from?' Further down, in rightfully dramatic sentences, it told how London, and especially the East of it, were set ablaze by ninety minutes of falling bombs and fire fighting.

From nowhere came a chirpy voice with a winning smile, 'Well, if it isn't the young golden crusaders – what on earth are you doing in here this early?'

'Hello Mr Ruby,' they both said wearily, looking round. 'We're just doing some research 'cos my computer has gone a bit *plum*.' Jack knew that switching off the screen now would look suspicious. Mr Ruby came over and stood over Jack's shoulder looking at their research.

'Gosh, the war eh? Fascinating stuff. Well, I read the paper at the weekend – saw you guys found more of that gold. Hey, you aren't looking for the rest of it, are you?'

'No way, Mr Ruby, we've learned our lesson. And we really were just on a visit to the Monument for no real reason,' said Wade a little defensively. Jack just nodded.

'Ah I see… well that's the papers for you, eh?'

'Actually, did we see you yesterday? By Stockwell Tube?' Wade asked a direct question.

'Me? No, 'fraid not. True, I do live around here, but I wasn't there yesterday morning.' Mr Ruby didn't seem phased by the question. 'So, what have you found out about the Blitz? It looks fascinating and who was this *Horatio Plum* fellow? He looks like a rascal for sure!' said Mr Ruby.

They stifled a snigger at his use of the word rascal.

'Well, we'll just carry on researching then.' Wade was trying to be as polite and respectful as possible.

'Can I help you with any of this – some good websites maybe?' Mr Ruby didn't get the hint as they both shook their heads. 'Ok. Hey, I wonder if there is any more gold. Bet you've got some ideas!' continued Mr Ruby enthusiastically. Wade shrugged his shoulders.

'Well not really. We're trying not to think about all of that; despite what the papers said, we're not really interested in any more of it. We made promises not to go looking,' said Wade.

'Are you sure?' he asked with a sad face. A few silent moments passed. 'Well, I guess you'll be looking forward to finishing school next week, then you'll have six weeks to go on more exciting adventures.'

'Well, sure, I guess. Ok then, we'll just be in here researching and stuff.' Wade turned back to the screen.

'Well make sure you don't go on any golden-goose hunts or decipher any secret messages!' Mr Ruby smiled. With one last look at the screen, he left.

'I think I convinced him,' said Wade with a hint of smugness.

'I know I'm always suspicious, but did you notice what he said there, at the end?' asked Jack.

'What – not to go looking for any of the leftover gold?'

'Yes, but it was the way he said it,' Jack said quietly, 'and how did he know we were in here? You know I didn't mention we'd thought we'd seen him yesterday *morning*.'

'Blimey, you *are* suspicious,' said Wade, although he took another moment to look around himself.

'So, we're closer to that gold now, eh?' said Wade later that day as they walked towards the park where Wade had evaded a UXB just a few months ago.

'A bit… but there's too many questions and I'm still suspic… concerned about who might be shadowing us and why. It's not right somehow.'

'Maybe someone will be at the café… or are they watching us *now*?' Wade made a spooky ghostly noise and laughed. 'Maybe that blackbird in the tree has a secret camera?' He laughed on as Jack just rolled his eyes.

Around eighty metres behind them walked a hooded man. He had a rucksack over his shoulder. Stepping behind a tree, he slowly reached into his bag. *Keep walking, Goldbusters, I'm coming for you both now.*

Just then, from the alleyway in front of them, Faiza walked towards Jack and Wade, giving a little wave.

'I bet she's got orders to make sure we go straight home,' mumbled Wade.

'Hmm, that might not be such a bad idea what with how things are right now,' replied Jack.

As if to add fuel to Jack's fears, Faiza came closer and whispered, 'Don't look now, but I think someone's following you.'

17

'Let's stop and see what he does,' whispered Wade.

Jack nodded, then dropped his own rucksack to the ground and, as before, pretended to look for something in it. Anyone within earshot would have heard Faiza and Wade moan at him for not finding it. Jack looked through Wade's legs and spotted a hooded man around a hundred metres back partially hidden by a tree.

'Who is it?' said Wade as he pretended to be cross at Jack.

'Not sure, can't see all of his face – looks like someone in a blue hoodie, standing by a tree. What should we do?' replied Jack.

'I'll tell you what we do – we go and have a chat with him!' said Faiza walking towards the figure. Wade and Jack followed rapidly. The man, now just fifty metres away from Faiza, did a slight double-take and, looking around himself, quickly headed off. Faiza stopped and shouted after the man, who just carried on running and disappeared down the alleyway. Faiza shouted something else unintelligible and marched back to Wade and Jack, still mumbling under her breath.

'Do you think that was Mr—' Wade started to ask as someone behind them in a brown suede jacket suddenly said.

'Hello, you two, *again…* oh, and hello, Miss Saab – the *Goldbusters* all together again? Are you sure you're not hunting for any extra hidden gold?' Mr Ruby smiled his disarming smile.

The three looked stunned for a second.

'Hello, Mr – erm – Ruby. *Again.* How are you?' Wade said with a slightly exasperated sigh.

'Fine thanks. Was that you shouting, Miss Saab?' He looked at Faiza who met his gaze. 'Was that a friend of yours, that man in the hoodie?'

'No idea. Actually, there was a dog and I wanted it to go away… don't like dogs,' she said flatly.

Mr Ruby looked past her but saw nothing. 'What are you three all doing then? I saw the boys earlier and they were adamant they weren't doing anything dodgy.'

'Nothing,' Wade and Faiza said together, a little too quickly.

'We're just heading home after a tough day at school. Is this your way home too?' added Wade.

Mr Ruby shook his head. 'No, I was just out walking after a busy day at school. Lots of SLT meetings and parents. I'll be off now then. Stay safe.' He took one more look past them and headed off across the grass to the right.

In an unoccupied back garden, the man in the blue hoodie crouched by a shed getting his breath back. *Who the hell was that brown suede person? I'm sick of following… time to be strategic and use what I know.* He paused. *Oh, this is going to be good.* He got up, dusted himself down and headed out of the garden. Cautiously he slunk down the alley away from the park, his mind full of scheming.

The three walked slowly on. Checking around them, Wade said, 'What's an SLT?' Getting no answer, he added, 'Is anyone else following us?'

'No, I don't think so,' said Jack looking around too. 'I think he, or they, have gone.'

'I could just be paranoid, and I only saw part of his face, but I'm sure I've seen that blue-hooded man somewhere before, though I can't place him,' said Faiza.

'And why was Mr Ruby *here*?' said Jack, clearly more exasperated. 'And why do we keep on bumping into him?'

'He does seem to be a bit of a bad smell – we can't get rid of him!' laughed Faiza.

'They definitely weren't the same person then?' asked Wade.

'No, apart from the fact they were different heights, build and jacket colour, Ruby couldn't have made it round from the far side of the park to behind us in seven seconds,' replied Jack matter-of-factly.

'I've seen Wade run faster when it's time to do the housework,' quipped Faiza.

Sitting at the café ten minutes later, Wade tucked into a burger. Jack looked around himself holding a glass of cola as Faiza sipped a cup of Earl Grey Tea.

'So, I did a bit of research myself today and… but, look, you guys go first,' she said.

'Well, we started off by looking at the pictures and trying to cross-link them with the documents that—' said Wade.

'Oh, blah blah blah – just the facts, geekoids,' Faiza cut in a little tersely. 'Which station is the *ng* from?'

'If I may, the *ng* we saw must be Charing Cross. It fits exactly – close to Plum and near the Monument, easy to get to.' Jack smiled. 'And of course, CC in that code could simply be Charing Cross.'

'Trouble was, the picture didn't fit what Charing Cross looks like, which stumped us at first,' chirped in Wade.

'Yes, we weren't thinking laterally. We needed a little more temporal thought,' mused Jack.

'That'll be the phase inducers next to the Tachyon beam then? Seriously, what are you talking about?' Faiza rolled her eyes.

Jack gave a sheepish smile. 'Oh yes, sorry, well, by temporal, I mean time,' he replied to continuingly nonplussed looks. 'I laid the picture on an *old* map of the Underground.' Jack showed a picture of the teardrop and then flipped to a page from his *Historical London* app. They all squinted at the screen, which showed an Underground map from 1938.

'Superb, and that means that the teardrop is the shape of the old abandoned Northern Line tunnels under the Thames that stretch out from what used to be called Charing Cross Station and is now called Embankment Station – look, it fits on that old map of the Underground!'

'Only problem is, I wonder what the rest of it means. The NL 09 126S?'

'When you two have quite finished celebrating your bromance club, I think you'll find I can answer that,' said Faiza, with more than a hint of smugness.

They both looked at her with a happily surprised look on their faces.

'Yep, me,' she continued. 'I know it's usually your job, *brainbox*.' She looked at Jack. 'But this time I might have it. I think those numbers mean how far along the track to go – 126 S is obviously 126 steps along the southbound Northern Line.' They looked impressed. 'I spent some of today looking at loads of Underground stuff on one of the school tablets.' There was a deserved smugness to her voice.

'We're so much closer and we can get started straight away by going to Embankment! How about taking a day off school and going there tomorrow?' said Wade excitedly.

Jack and Faiza were less enthusiastic.

'I don't think so to be honest,' said Faiza after a few moments' silence. 'I'm not sure and that's what I was saying yesterday – I think we should let things cool for a bit. Being followed and hassled and threatened just shows I'm right. This morning, Janet said…'

'Janet?! But we're so close – we now know where it is,' argued Wade.

'Where it *might* be. Wade, it's just not a clever idea right now. Corner is right – we seem to be attracting attention everywhere,' countered Jack.

'Oh, come on, cos we're *pesky kids,* we can fit in anywhere,' said Wade over-optimistically.

Jack frowned – that one dismissive statement concealed the danger they could be facing.

'Look, we keep ending up in this situation and I've had such hassle from my mum, and your dad's giving you grief – I heard it last night!' explained Faiza.

Wade looked a little embarrassed. Jack nodded slowly – he knew his own parents had given him a tough time for yet again getting into a '*right dangerous mess*' as his dad had called it.

'So, we just give up? We just give up on all that lovely gold out there and we know where it is?' Wade replied, looking at the horizon. 'That's ours and we're going to find it first – with all of us together we can—'

'Give it a rest, bro,' cut in Faiza. 'We've got some theories, but we just seem to be getting deeper and deeper! Let's leave it for a while.'

'Hrummph,' Wade exclaimed. He knew better than to argue with Faiza. Maybe he could persuade Jack? 'Jack – come on, what do you think? We're SO close!'

'We're really not. I think we need to face facts. We've found some of the gold already… and who knows, maybe Embankment does hold the key. All we know for sure is things happen to people who go after that gold. It feels like there are strange threatening people everywhere, literally. I actually think Miss Corner is understating it; it really *is* dangerous.' He expected protests or jibes from Wade or even Faiza, but both sat listening as he continued. 'Look, why don't we knock all this on the head and wait for the heat to fade… just for now?'

Faiza nodded slowly, 'I think that's the most you've ever said… *Jack*,' she said smiling. 'Nicely said. He's right, Wade. Come on – let's leave it for now and come back to it after the heat has died down… after the holidays maybe.'

Wade looked at her, then Jack, with an expression of tetchiness which melted into resignation. 'Ugh, really?' Wade eventually said flatly. He sighed loudly. 'But promise me we'll keep all the stuff we've got and go looking again once we think it's safe?'

Jack and Faiza nodded, and Jack put his arm round Wade's shoulders. 'It'll be alright, mate, it's been there over eighty odd years already – wherever that gold is, it's going nowhere anytime soon.'

18

As a result of deciding to take it easy, their last few days of the term were less of an anxious slog and much more of a cheerful time. They were nearly famous again, for a day: almost two, but not to nearly the same degree as before. There was the promise of interviews: one radio and two newspapers but not much more. They weren't even asked onto *Lorraine*! Wade was the least happy of all of them at this.

Once they had made the decision to stop looking for trouble, they felt it had stopped looking for them. There were a few times when they were heading to or from school that they felt they might be being watched, but, after seeing no-one, decided it was just nerves or imagination. Mr Ruby was as curious and attentive as usual, but they just acted nonchalantly and, after some social niceties, he would disappear. The last day rolled around and their form tutor, Mrs. Poppet, was finishing her end-of-year monologue.

'...and finally, I would like to thank you all, well most of you anyway, for making this year a most interesting one.' Mrs. Poppet looked directly at Wade and Jack.

A voice from the back. 'Miss, can I take the pencils and glitter glue since we're leaving?'

There was an audible groan from the rest of the class.

'No, Justin. Could someone take him out of here please?' sighed Mrs. Poppet. 'I'll make sure your new teacher, Mr Ruby, knows all about you.' With a wave of her hand and some slightly hysterical laughter, she dismissed class 8P for the last time.

Wade and Jack made their goodbyes to their friends with promises to message them every day, and then joined the loud throng of teenagers leaving school on the final day of term.

'Right, that's Year Eight done, now what?' said Jack happily. 'Six weeks of glorious doing-nothingness awaits!'

'Hoh yes!' exclaimed Wade. 'Hey and guess what – I've got tickets to go and visit one of those Underground tours you're always banging on about!'

'Oh wow, which one?' asked Jack excitedly.

'The Post Office Mail Rail one!' said Wade looking pleased with himself.

'Wow, they're hard to come by. You usually have to book months in advance – how did you get them?'

'I got a message from my dad earlier saying they'd come in as a prize.'

'A prize?' Jack frowned. 'That's unusual – what else did he say?'

'Ah, just that we're all going tomorrow. Great, eh?'

'Yeah, that's brilliant – I've already looked at the map of Post Office tunnels; so much of it is closed to the public! Wimpole Street, Western Central, Rathbone Place!'

'Blimey, do you know *all* the stations on the Underground?' laughed Wade.

'Who doesn't?' Jack shrugged, then added, 'So, what time are we going?'

'Erm, it's just for four apparently so the family – erm,' said Wade looking a little sheepish.

'Ah… yeah… of course. Sure. It's ok, I know what that's like. Look, you have a great time and tell me all about it!' Jack said quickly, covering up a deflated feeling.

'Yeah, it's for tomorrow,' continued Wade, 'but look, we can meet after if you like?'

'Yeah sure, why not.' Jack was definitely less impressed.

At 11:34 on the first day of the summer holidays, Faiza, Wade and their parents – Nida and Dexter – were gathered in the Postal Museum in North London. They stood with a dozen other people by a small odd-looking red train which had a perspex roof. After getting there early, they had spent forty-five minutes in the museum trying on old mail outfits and looking at how mail had been delivered by all manner of transport. Wade had even bought an old-style postbag with a *W* on the front.

'Jack would say how this was all superfluous with email and instant messaging,' said Wade knowingly.

'That's amazing!' said Faiza.

'What is?'

'That you know what superfluous means!' Faiza smiled.

'Faiza,' warned her mum in a low tone. 'Play nice.'

'You're right, Mum – we'll just have to get through the day without Wade's geeky shadow.'

'How long do we have to wait, Dad?' asked Wade, ignoring Faiza.

'The tickets say 11:45, for the eighth time.' His dad sighed as he rolled his eyes at Nida.

'Were they top prize?' Wade persisted.

'No idea – I got them in an email. Apparently, they're giving them away to celebrate some anniversary or other – I checked: all legit tickets!' replied his dad, moving Wade forward.

'Guess I was just lucky,' he added.

Wade frowned as he munched on some chocolate – he had learned from Jack to be suspicious of gift horses.

A woman in an old postmaster uniform stepped out from the red train and motioned for them all to move forward. 'Welcome all! Many people do not even know there is a secret Underground railway that used to carry mail across London from over a hundred years ago,' she began. 'It's made up of six and a half miles of tunnels at an average of seventy feet below ground. In the early twentieth century…' Wade tuned out at this point and munched on another chocolate; he just wanted to get on the miniature train and get going. He peered down into the end of the tunnel and into darkness. Four minutes later, the woman ushered them on board.

As his parents got into one of the small carriages, Wade pulled Faiza into the one next to it and they sat down. The small door at shin level clicked shut quietly. Luckily the roof and windows were transparent. Each of the small carriages was separate from each other and he waved and made faces at his dad through the perspex window.

As the miniature train launched into action, the recorded voice came over the intercom and announced more facts about the narrow-gauge railway. The lights of the museum faded and, after a moment of darkness, the bright but temporary ceiling lights lit the way, giving the place a kind of unreal feeling. The tube tunnels were almost familiar, being just a little smaller and a lot cleaner than might usually be found on the main network. As the train trundled forward, Wade could see lots of phone screens lit up taking pictures of anything that did and didn't move.

A few minutes later they pulled into the platform under Mount Pleasant Sorting Office which, according to the announcer, 'was very busy for decades and even had its own dartboard'. They also watched a short presentation displayed on the tunnel wall telling of the history of the Mail Rail over the last ten decades.

'You're loving this, eh?' said Faiza, turning round to Wade as he stared out the windows taking it all in. Wade just nodded as the train moved on with further announcements from the intercom. Less than a minute had passed when the train jerked to a halt and the lights all went out.

'What's happening?' Faiza asked.

Wade didn't reply and, in the darkness, came some clicking noises and shuffling. Breaking the silence, the intercom crackled loudly, and the voice offered apologies and confirmed there had been a slight technical fault.

'Still loving this?' Faiza asked Wade.

Again, there was no reply. Faiza turned towards Wade to find he was not there.

19

Faiza tried to stand up and banged her head on the perspex roof. Sitting back down, she looked around feeling a growing sense of panic. In the half-light, it was hard to make out anything but shadows. She called Wade's name loudly and people in the other train carriages looked in her direction.

'Faiza, what are you doing?' hissed Nida anxiously from her carriage.

'It's Wade – he's not here!' she replied loudly, trying to get out and finding the small door was being very obstinate.

'Wade? Wade boy, where are you? Stop mucking about!' said Wade's dad urgently – he banged the windows and shouted Wade's name. The door to their carriage didn't open either.

Other people started calling his name or tutting and asking what was wrong. The intercom burst into life and the lady asked people to sit down and relax, adding that the train would be on the move again soon. Faiza stared out of the window and towards a side tunnel. A few metres further down in the semi-darkness, her eyes rested on a small bag emblazoned with a *W* – Wade's bag.

With renewed effort, Faiza managed to prise open the

small door a little. She contorted and squeezed her way through the angry doors and ducked out along the passage. The doors snapped shut and behind her she could hear muffled shouts to 'come back'. The train suddenly lurched away and the noises from the train grew smaller. In the side tunnel Faiza picked up Wade's bag. Further into the darkness, she was sure she could hear scuffling, so, treading carefully, she made her way through the unusual terrain to a recess in the wall.

Following the sounds, Faiza pushed open a large wooden door and slipped through. This thin curved tunnel was clearly once a storage area with piles of bolts and wooden sleepers. It had pale lights every few metres that looked like they had been strung up in a hurry. She was about to call out for Wade when she heard a deeper muffled voice from further round the bend. The voice seemed to be repeating, 'No, no.' There was some more indistinct shouting and then quiet.

Faiza stopped – had they heard her? Just then the lights went out and she held her breath. The only thing she could hear was the deafening silence. She breathed out slowly. As lightly as she could, she tentatively edged through the tunnel. She jumped in the next moment as the lights came back on and, ahead of her, she could hear more indistinct noises. She had to get to Wade and quickly.

About ten metres in front of her, she could make out a hooded Wade on the floor; he was alone and still. Next to him was a mound of equipment and some safety clothes. She ran the short distance and looked him up and down. She pulled the hood off his head, and he groaned and opened his eyes.

'Are you ok? What happened?' she asked, brushing some dust off his face.

'I don't know. I was sitting there, and some bloke picked me up and ran,' he mumbled, lifting his head up.

'You look alright apart from that ugly mug – how many fingers do I have up?' She gave him a V sign.

He rolled his eyes and groaned again as he pulled himself to his feet. 'Very funny. Ugh, my head hurts!' he moaned, as he rubbed it with his left hand.

'What happened—' she started before stopping suddenly. Looking horrified and letting out a little shriek of alarm, she looked at him, then his hand, which was covered in blood.

'What?' he said, confused, before his eyes settled on his red hand. It was his turn to shriek. He quickly checked himself – he didn't think he had any cuts, so where was the blood coming from?

With rising panic, he stepped back into the light and fell over the pile of equipment and clothes. Faiza went to help Wade to his feet and he stood there a little shakily looking intently at his hand and mumbling about falling over. Faiza examined his hand and noticed that the blood was not just on Wade's hand. There seemed to be a few spots on his shoes and on the ground leading to the pile of safety clothes to her left.

She tentatively pulled a yellow vest back and picked up a bloodied knife that sat gleaming underneath it. She ran it over in her hands and checked Wade again – relieved to find no wounds at all. Confused, she gently pulled back a few red safety helmets and fell back in terror. Wade moved forward to see what Faiza had seen and held his breath – in front of them was the body of a man with a bloodied gash in his orange Hi-viz. There was more blood down his front and around his mouth. His eyes were open, and he was still.

20

Both Faiza and Wade stood in horror, unable to move, staring at the immobile body.

'Is he… It wasn't… I didn't… is he…?' said Wade forcing the words out.

'What?! Look at him… What did you… did you? What happened?!' hissed Faiza dropping the knife. It landed with a soft clatter. They barely noticed as from further round the bend came the noise of people approached. Wade went to open his mouth, but Faiza shook her head.

'We've got to get out of here now. NOW!' she hissed. Pulling a resistant Wade, they ran and stumbled further into the darkness.

Several second later, two men in bright orange vests came around the corner. Their voices came loudly and angrily.

'Hey you – stop there, get back here!'

'We've called the Transport Police – there's no way out, get back here, it's dangerous!'

The man at the front stopped suddenly by the pile of clothes and equipment. He pulled his colleague closer.

'Blimey! Colin, look here – someone's dead – they've killed someone!'

'What are you wittering about, Lorram, it can't—' The other man suddenly swore and pulled his radio out.

'Charlie Tango, it's Colin – get the BTP here quick. We've got a dead body here – stabbed. Two youth suspects legged it. We need a lockdown now!'

Further up the tunnel, Faiza and Wade realised that the security men were right – the tunnel did indeed come to a dead end. There were some small alcoves, but no way out. Against the back wall was a large metal cage containing a very neat array of cones, coils of rope and electric cable. The place was in darkness apart from a long strip light at the back of the cage. They could see the door was unlocked with an open padlock hanging from the gate. Wade and Faiza listened in fear as they heard the two security men coming closer. Wade clicked his fingers and pointed at the tidy equipment.

Less than thirty seconds later, the two men came bounding round the corner and stopped in front of the cage. They looked stumped for a moment.

'Where are they?' blurted Lorram frustratedly.

Colin peered into the cage and nudged his colleague. He pointed specifically at the untidy coils in the corner which were now on their sides and covered by cones. Carefully, Colin pulled the door open and went in as Lorram stood at the cage entrance. From an alcove to the left came a whooshing sound, followed by an 'oof' as Lorram went flying into the cage, landing heavily on Colin. Wade jumped up out of the other alcove and slammed the door as Faiza closed the padlock, locking the gate. Colin managed to push Lorram off and tried to open the gate. He shouted at Faiza and Wade as they quickly headed back down the tunnel to the sound of the gate being rattled uselessly.

Some thirty metres from where Colin and Lorram were barking at each other in confused shock, Wade and Faiza sat breathing heavily in the darkness. They had run back and dived into a side tunnel before cutting back across the main tracks. At one point, Wade almost stopped to look at children's drawings on the wall before heading into another tunnel which branched off to the left. Now they had their backs against a metal gate which stretched across the whole width of the tunnel that just seemed to lead to more darkness. There was a warning on the gate forbidding entrance and almost threatening death to anyone who dared to try and pass through it.

'What the hell just happened, Wade?' asked Faiza urgently once they were sure they were not followed. 'What did you do?'

'What? I didn't do *that*!' he replied indignantly.

'Well of course you didn't – you get nervous if you have to shoo a fly from the room! Just tell me what happened,' she said, pulling her scarf tighter.

'So, I was looking out of the window when it went dark and we slowed down. Suddenly I was grabbed by someone. They put a coat or sack over me, and I was pulled through the doors. Then I was being carried along the tunnel. I couldn't shout or anything – good job you came after me.'

'Well yeah, I found your bag and managed to follow you,' cut in Faiza.

'Thank God – so he dumped me where you found me, but I still couldn't see. Then there was scuffling, and someone shouted "*No no*" and I heard helmets and stuff being kicked before it all went quiet.'

'So, you didn't see him or who attacked him?'

'No, I still had my head covered. I don't know who he was… and now he's dead!' Wade's voice wavered.

'Maybe we should have stayed there… I thought it was someone coming back to get *us*.'

'No, you were right,' replied Wade. 'We had to get out of there.' He reached into his pocket and pulled out a chocolate, offering Faiza one. She took one and munched on it meaningfully.

'Mum and Dad will be going mad – we should maybe head back and tell them the truth?' Faiza said. Somewhere in the tunnels close by they could hear shouting and footfalls, and a flashlight would briefly light up the cross tunnel in front of them before going dark again.

'Back? Back to that? No way. Look at me – you know I'll get the blame for it,' said Wade anxiously.

'Me too,' added Faiza sadly. 'They'll think we both did it!'

'We have to get out of here!' Wade sounded more than a little perturbed.

'I know you didn't do that, squib,' she said sympathetically, 'but think: how will we get out and where will we go?'

Indistinct noises seemed to get louder from the tunnels they had run through. Suddenly, Wade stood up and pulled at the gate, but it held fast thanks to a large rusty padlock. Next to him Faiza tried as well with the same result: this gate was going nowhere. Wade frowned and suddenly scrambled up the gate and managed to edge between the top of it and the tunnel roof. He laughed and landed the other side, beckoning for Faiza to join him. Faiza's slim frame and longer legs meant that she found it slightly easier, and she landed beside him. He rolled his eyes as she gave a smug smile. After briefly looking behind at the growing lights, they ran and were swallowed up in the darkness, leaving nothing but footprints and a chocolate wrapper.

21

'Where does it lead to? Where can we get out?' whispered Faiza a few minutes later as they walked forward in the semi-darkness. The tunnel now seemed to be on a slightly downward slope and was illuminated every twenty metres or so by a strip light hanging either from the ceiling or loosely strapped to the wall. Dust and dirt clung to every surface and the air was musty and cool.

'There were a few stations on that map, but they're not open to the public – I think the next one is *Western Central*. Jack mentioned it yesterday as well.'

'Of course he did,' replied Faiza rolling her eyes. 'So how far is it?'

'Not sure – probably about half an hour's walk.' Wade coughed; the air was musty and dry. They carefully trod along the tracks avoiding the rails. Even though they knew the current was off, they weren't taking any chances.

Another quarter of an hour passed with Wade and Faiza making their way carefully but with a sense of urgency through the tunnels.

'I don't like this – it's one of the weirdest things hearing rumbling trains somewhere above or to your side. As long as they don't come down this tunnel,' said Wade as he munched on another chocolate.

'I don't like it either, you know, and it's your fault, you know. There we were happily on a tour, and *you* go and decide to get involved in murdering someone.'

'Well, *you* discovered the body and it was *you* that had the knife; maybe it was *you*?' Wade teased.

'Ugh, I'm getting stalactites in my hair,' said Faiza rubbing her head.

'An improvement for sure,' quipped Wade.

'You're the one that looks better in the dark. Keep moving.' She pushed him forward.

A minute later and Wade pointed further up the track.

'I think we're getting close to a station – it's going uphill again. I suppose it's to decelerate a train.'

'Wow *decelerate*, guess all that talking nonsense with Jack is making you almost clever,' she said, adding, 'Just watch out for those tracks and points.'

As they walked forward, the whole place became brighter and better lit. They edged slowly past an abandoned Mail Rail train which clearly hadn't been used for a very long time and a yellow and black sign that announced *12.205.*

'We'll have to keep moving – who knows whether anyone followed us this far,' said Faiza looking around herself anxiously.

'We need to contact Jack and let him know everything: he'll have a good idea about that dead body,' added Wade seriously.

'He'd probably tell us to hand ourselves in since we didn't actually do *it*,' replied Faiza.

'If only we could phone him, or he could track us or something,' said Faiza sadly. She looked at her mobile and was amazed to see it had one bar of signal.

Wade suddenly stopped and hissed, 'Oh no, *track*! Quick, turn your phone off – when it gets a signal, they'll be able to track us!'

'How do you know – oh of course, I guess you and *chief of geeks* talk about that sort of stuff all the time.' Faiza quickly switched off her phone as Wade shrugged and did the same.

'No, no – actually I saw it on a rerun of *Torchwood* the other day.'

Faiza looked at him and shook her head.

Twenty metres further on and they stepped up onto the deserted platform. It looked like it had just been left and forgotten. Dirty broken ladders, trolleys and coils of cable littered the place. Above them was a suspended ceiling and there were now several holes in it where plastic panels had come down. A sign on the wall announced it was *Western Central Sorting Office*.

'Wow, this is like a time capsule – think of what we could find here!' enthused Wade.

'No time to look around this time,' stated Faiza. 'Let's get out of here.' She ushered a protesting Wade towards the main doorway but they both stopped in front of it. The whole doorway was bricked up, sealing the station off from the outside world. They ran further along the platform and were dismayed to find it was the same with the two other doorways. Wade was about to ask what they should do now, when he saw something that made him smile: a grey wall-mounted telephone looked out at them almost beckoning them to use it.

'Is that a telephone?' Faiza asked incredulously, but Wade was already dialling Jack's number.

'It's working, it's working!' he exclaimed excitedly. Then: 'Oh.' Jack's mobile had gone straight through to voicemail, but they didn't leave a message. Wade then dialled Jack's landline. It took a long time for the ringing tone which followed some distant strange clicks on the line. 'Hello, is Jack there? It's Wade.'

'Actually, I'm afraid not,' came a man's voice. 'He's recently gone out.' There was a pause, then: 'Where are you, Wade?'

'Oh, hi Mr Roble, I was just getting home, and I wondered if he could join us?'

'He did leave a message if you rang. He said to tell you that *he was off like the clappers to the place before the old jail and after the oranges*… does that make sense, Wade? Sounds very odd, do you know where he is?'

'No, no idea,' replied Wade flatly. 'He likes being cryptic. I'll call him later. If he comes back, please tell him I'm off home.'

'You could always come here and wait? No, ok… take care, young man.'

'Thanks, Mr Roble. Bye.' Wade put the phone down and ushered Faiza into a recessed cubicle. 'Something wrong there – Mr Roble doesn't usually ask me in to wait and definitely wouldn't ask me where I was calling from.'

'You think he's got *company*? Maybe someone's already trying to get us,' Faiza suggested.

'There were a few strange noises on the phone before it connected – what if someone was listening in?'

'We'd better get going… what else did he say?'

'He gave me an odd message from Jack.' Wade was about to retell the message when he heard something that made them both stop dead. There were scuffling noises and shouting coming from further back along the tunnel – someone was following them and getting closer.

22

'We've got to move!' Faiza quickly grabbed one of the dilapidated ladders and pushed it against the wall under one of the holes in the fake ceiling. As Wade watched, she pinned her scarf onto the top of the ladder.

'You owe me a silk scarf. Anyway, it might slow them for a while,' she whispered as they jumped off the platform and headed further into the tunnels.

'Who wears a silk scarf on an Underground tour?' asked Wade.

'It's called fashion – you should try it one day,' she smirked.

'Yeah, because that's really important down here. Often see the rats in a floral top looking for a silk scarf,' he remarked deadpan.

'Shut up or I'm leaving you down here with those rats.'

They walked much faster now and, so far, there seemed to be no noise immediately behind them. Dust and ancient equipment seemed to be everywhere as well as flecks of white paint that had fallen from the ceiling.

'How did they find us?' asked Wade a few minutes later, moving fast along the tunnels and munching his last chocolate.

'Tell me you didn't leave any of those anywhere,' said

Faiza pointing at a wrapper he held in his hand. Wade looked a little sheepish and shook his head.

'I know when you're lying! Oh great, so now they're following your wrappers like Hansel and Gretel?'

'Well,' he started, 'I *may* have dropped one or two… doesn't mean they can track us.' He gave a pleading smile. Faiza was about to find something to throw at him when Wade pointed ahead and said excitedly, 'Look, another station!'

They climbed onto the platform at a station identified as *Rathbone Place*.

'If Jack was here, he'd probably tell us the history of this place,' said Wade, looking around impressed.

'Yeah, like how the motors are formed of barium quantum-shift turbines and can be phase-induced with a power signature of 1.21 gigawatts,' replied Faiza, laughing, as they made their way along the dusty platform.

'Ha ha, yeah. Hey look – here!' Although the doorways were blocked off like the previous station, the bricks at the bottom of the furthermost fire exit had crumbled, but the gap was too small to get through. They looked at each other as again they could hear noises from further up the tunnel. Working as a team, they quickly pulled at the surrounding bricks so there was a gap large enough for each one of them to get through.

'Ugh, look at my jacket,' moaned Wade as he eased through the small hole – it was now coated in an oil and dirty water mix and it had a strange unpleasant smell.

'At last, you're looking cool, even if you do smell a bit funky,' she laughed as they began to make it look like the whole place had been undisturbed. They headed up the well-lit metal circular staircase which snaked around a metal chute, once used for transporting sacks of mail down to the platform. Their footsteps clanked on the metal steps despite walking as silently as they could.

At the top, they stood a little breathlessly in front of a metal door. A metal bar was across the door with a heavy padlock at one end. Wade pulled at it and surprisingly the padlock was rusted open. He pulled it and then slid the bar into the edging and both were amazed to find the door creaked open a little. There was a slight gust of stale air and, after so long in the semi-darkness, the light felt blinding. They were in bright sunshine, a welcome change to the dark claustrophobia they had just escaped through.

'Where have we come out?' asked Wade pushing through the door. There was a crash as he stumbled over some old tarpaulins and damp cardboard boxes.

'More importantly, where do we go?' Faiza said, stepping over the boxes and Wade. They seemed to be in the bottom of another stairwell, this one much dirtier and smellier than where they had been. The door slammed shut behind them making them both jump.

'No way back then,' said Faiza sadly, noting the lack of a handle this side of the door.

'And no-one waiting for us.' Wade breathed a sigh of relief then frowned at his increasingly smelly clothes. They cautiously walked up the mildewed concrete stairs to another doorway which led to a paved and grassed area. There were lots of people walking about, but happily they took scant notice of the two. Heading to the left, they came out onto a main road. A sign indicated that they had just been in *Rathbone Square W1*. Wade pointed at the BT Tower glinting in the sunlight.

'Wow look where we are!' he said excitedly.

Almost a mile away, in a coffee shop close to the Postal Museum, a man in a long grey coat received a message on his phone. He frowned. *How could they have got away? I dragged that boy to the body and, thanks to my contacts, it should have been foolproof. Obviously, my friends bumbled it. I am sick of this tomfoolery – if you've got to do some-thing, do it yourself. I'm going to end this now.* He grabbed his rucksack and headed out of the coffee shop. Seventeen seconds later, a man in the same coffee shop put on his red baseball cap and made a call.

'We'll have to keep moving – who knows if anyone fol-lowed us,' said Faiza looking around herself anxiously, then added, 'What was Jack's message?'

Wade told Faiza the whole of Jack's perplexing mes-sage: *off like the clappers to the place before the old jail and after the oranges.*

'Do you think the old jail might be the Clink?' asked Wade.

A few moments of them frowning passed as they both headed further down Newman Street, trying to look inconspicuous and being alert at the same time. Faiza clicked her fingers and leaned into Wade.

'We're sticking out like sore thumbs. Let's split up – I'll see you in M & S at LB – in half an hour?' Without wait-ing for confirmation, she disappeared over the road and into the crowd leaving a slightly perplexed Wade.

23

Why does everyone talk in code? Wade thought as he stood in the doorway for a minute, running over the last part of the conversation in his mind. His face lit up as he realised what Faiza had meant. A police car with lights flashing passed and he quickly looked hard at a shop window. It stopped two hundred metres back up the road where they had come out. Keeping his head down, he crossed Oxford Street and headed into the back streets.

It was thirty-eight minutes later when the escalator Wade was on emerged onto the bright London Bridge concourse. He had been very careful and taken a non-direct route to get here. His anti-following methods had also involved back-tracking once or twice and jumping on and off trains at the last moment to confuse any would-be follower. The concourse was bright and looked modern, with its electronic indicator boards and large LCD screen with news clips and adverts.

Keeping a low profile, he headed for where Faiza had mentioned. He hoped he had worked it out right. Stopping near the doors, Wade felt that everyone was looking at him at first but knew that they were all looking at the times of their next and cancelled services. He looked past them at the electronic gates. The area was big and open, and anyone could easily find anyone, which in turn meant anyone could spot him or Faiza. Was this where Jack had meant and where was he anyway?

Still acting nonchalantly, he walked back from the doors and went into the retail area. As he did so, someone tugged at his jacket. He looked round and heard a whisper.

'Sit down and start drinking this.' Faiza smiled from under a hat indicating the drink and seat in front of her. 'Glad you're ok even if you are late,' she said.

Breathing a sigh of relief, Wade smiled and sat down. 'Where's Jack? Is he here?' he asked, taking a slurp of the fizzy drink and looking suspiciously at the table waiter nearby.

'No, he's not here – this was just so we could get out of there quickly. Well done on getting here.'

'I got it. Hey, where did you get that jacket and hat?' asked Wade. She was now sporting a white jacket and a beret.

'Just some little shop off Oxford Street – I used cash. Right, put your jacket in the bin and put this on.' She indicated a bag by her feet. Looking around, he reached into the bag and pulled out a brown jacket with tassels around the chest and elbows.

'Shut up – I'm not wearing that; I am *not* country and western,' he hissed.

'Wade, we *have* to do this. There's CCTV everywhere and we're being hunted. We *have to* look different, and this was all they had,' she replied. The way she said *have to* made Wade realise she was right. He sighed out loud and stroppily took off his jacket and put the tasselled leather one on. She handed him a wide-brimmed black hat and smiled.

'You did this on purpose,' he grumbled, making a face like he could smell something bad.

'No, honestly – it's all they had in your size. Go on, it suits you,' she encouraged. It was a good fit, he admitted to himself but still sat back frowning. 'I thought about Jack's message – I think I've worked it out,' Faiza said cheerfully and Wade's frown changed to a smile.

'Come on then!' complained Wade. But Faiza wasn't listening, she was staring at something over Wade's shoulder. Wade turned around, fearful of what he would see. He was right to be worried.

Across the other side of the concourse on the large electronic advertising screen, they were showing news highlights. Shockingly, these highlights were pictures of Wade and Faiza with the white and red news lettering exclaiming – *Hunt for murder suspects*. There was no volume, but the slightly delayed subtitles were clear: *...hunt is on for two suspects wanted in connection with a suspicious death earlier today at the Underground Postal Service.*

The background pictures changed to an image of the mail train and some members of the public leaving the train area. There were several policemen, standing around looking determined, alongside the obligatory Hi-Viz vest wearers. A policeman, with a nametag that said *Constable Stone* came on screen. *Yes, we have identified two youths we wish to help us with enquiries regarding a body found on the Post Office Mail Rail. They set off into the tunnels and we need to trace them urgently. We would ask the public to be vigilant and not to approach them but to call the number on screen.* A central London number appeared on screen. *We believe they are somewhere on the Underground network, and they are being actively sought there now.*

The policeman was replaced by a man in an orange

Hi-Viz vest with a bruise on his forehead. *I was the first there and I saw two youths by a dead body and one of them was holding a knife. They threatened us with it, but we chased the perpetrators. We almost got them, but after a physical assault they vanished in the tunnels.*

The newscaster's image appeared again alongside the pictures of Wade and Faiza. *The name of the dead person has been withheld until the next of kin have been notified. The youths' parents are helping the police with their enquiries.*

The screen changed yet again to an advert – this time for *Viking Milk.*

'That's not true – we didn't threaten them with a knife!' said Faiza angrily. Wade realised he was breathing quickly and turned back round to Faiza.

'We have to get out of here,' he hissed.

'Now you see why we need a disguise. Right look – follow me, separately. We're going to meet Jack. Walk towards... towards the market the long way round. Keep an eye on me... if we get separated... pray.' She got up and headed away without another word.

Wade got up mumbling about who put her in charge. He dropped the bag containing his old jacket into the bin.

'So is our whole life going to revolve around *this* station?' he said to himself grabbing the hat and following Faiza.

Six minutes later a man in a long grey coat approached the café area and looked around suspiciously. *Where are they?* He got his phone out and after a few seconds of tapping an app called *Kate Low*, walked over to the bin, and pulled out the bag with Wade's jacket inside. *Damn, he must have found the tracker – I worked so hard to get that on his jacket when I dragged him along the tunnels.*

The man went through the pockets and then, from the

collar, he pulled out a small, matt-black patch about four centimetres long, with a raised black bubble in the centre. The man made a face, threw it all back in the bin and headed back into the station. *They can't be far from here... I'll access the CCTV in the control room and find out where they went...*

24

At almost the same time, some twelve miles to the east in a top security prison:

'We think we've got a shiny new update on your dismal threats,' Corner said in a slow Northern Irish drawl. The man's eyes widened momentarily before returning to a dead stare. 'Well, I say *we* – it wasn't really me; it was those *pesky kids* again. You know, the ones who so easily stopped you the first time.' She paused. Aside from a slight twitch, the man remained motionless.

Miss Corner continued, 'They did a strangely efficient job and I suspect they had some inside help. We asked them to leave it all alone of course, but you know how difficult they are to stop.'

'Did they do something terrible?' The man spoke so quietly that she wondered if she had imagined it.

'Sorry?' Miss Corner asked. The man shuffled in his seat a little.

'I mean, how are they, bless them? I hope they aren't doing terrible things like murdering people.'

'Well, thank you for telling me you knew about it – I never mentioned that they were in trouble. I think we're going to have to restrict you even more.' The man just shook his head and mumbled something under his breath.

'How did you know about it? I know you haven't been out of here and I doubt the wardens have told you. Triangulation and frequency monitoring show a call was made from your cell area just an hour ago, but we cannot trace the number called – possibly a burner mobile?' She scanned his face for any tell-tale signs that she was right, but Plum was too well trained for that. Instead, he just shook his head.

'But I will tell you something, *boss*…' Plum said, cocking his head to one side.

Miss Corner coughed. 'I'm not your boss – you lost that privilege when you decided to be a greedy, lying, deceitful scumbag.'

'As I said, here's something. One – I know all about what your amateur baby detectives are doing, but I can't help it if they come to a sticky end whilst doing dangerous things. If they sadly do, I guess they're not going to be a problem for either of us.' He sat back and smiled a greasy, smug grin.

Miss Corner frowned briefly, before sitting back and smiling. 'Let me assure you, Plum, that whoever is pursuing those kids will be the ones that come to a sticky end long before you get your not-so-secret revenge; we have ways of making sure of that. Now mull over that as you spend a few years in solitary.' She turned to the agent by the door. 'Put him in enforced solitary: no visitors, no calls, basic needs only.' Corner got up and tapped four times on the door. *Basic needs* meant bread and water and a bucket of water to wash in and to use as a toilet.

Plum looked perturbed at this. 'What? Hang on, you can't do that, you can't do that! I demand my rights!' he shouted.

Miss Corner turned around and held up one finger in front of his face. 'You lost those rights the day you betrayed me and your country. Don't make me have to sedate you as well.' She looked at the burly warden as he entered. 'I suspect he has hidden contraband – he needs a thorough body cavity search. A *very* thorough one.'

Without another word, she and the agent swept out of the room. The warden just smiled as Plum banged his free fist on the metal table.

25

Faiza was a hundred metres or so ahead on the opposite side of the street from Wade. He felt very conspicuous in his tasselled, tan leather jacket and black hat, but no-one really paid him much attention. Faiza's route seemed to defy logic; she didn't stay on one direction for any length of time. A few times she even doubled back on herself which momentarily threw Wade. *How does she know where she's going?* There was a sign towards Borough Market – *Was that where they were going?* She went under a railway bridge, entered the market, and was promptly lost in the crowd.

Wade panicked a little and headed in a minute later – where was she? Was this where Jack had meant to meet? It felt a little more threatening than last time although that was probably because every person could be a potential witness, a potential person who could put an end to their freedom. Faiza was nowhere. He wandered through, recalling the time when Mr Blue was chasing him. He had set off a fire alarm and escaped, thanks also to some very friendly stallholders. Now he continued trying to look as innocent as possible as he strolled out into the warm sunshine. Feeling frustrated, he was about to turn around and walk back in, when he remembered Faiza's last words to *pray* – there in front of him was Southwark Cathedral.

In contrast to the bright and noisy world outside, the cathedral inside was cool with just a gentle background hum of visitors. Wade dug into his pocket and put two coins into the collection barrel. Walking up the main aisle towards the majestic nave in front, Wade stroked a small black and white cat – called Hodge according to his collar – that curled around his leg. As he stood up, he spotted a figure with a beret on in one of the pews three rows from the front. He sat down beside her as she looked up.

'Yeehaw!' she said stifling a giggle. 'Glad you made it, *pardner.*'

'Shut up… I still think you did this on purpose.' He frowned. 'So why are we *here* and where is Jack?'

'Honestly – keep up. Remember he said *he was off like the clappers to the place before the old jail and after the oranges*? Well – the Clink is just up the road, and the oranges must mean those Hi-Viz wardens at London Bridge,' said Faiza matter-of-factly.

Wade nodded. 'Ah yes. Oh well, I knew that of course,' he said, 'but what about the clappers then?'

'The bells. The bells have clappers in them,' replied Faiza looking smug. 'Guess all that time I spent with you geekoids recently has been paying off, sadly.'

Wade just gave her a doubtful look and was about to reply that maybe she was starting to turn into him when someone behind Wade spoke.

'I think the Dolly Parton convention is next door,' said Jack, laughing as he sat down next to Wade. 'I am SO glad you made it here!' Jack was wearing his usual black hooded jacket and rucksack. 'I saw your names come up on the news and I knew it was serious – I just grabbed my stuff, told my dad and I was out of there. Had to find you!'

'Thanks, mate', replied Wade. 'We got your message and worked it out.'

'Ahem,' said Faiza, '*who* worked it out?'

'*We* figured it out,' said Wade quickly.

'So,' said Jack looking at them both laughing, 'which one of you did it?'

Wade explained everything that had happened, with Faiza assisting when Wade lapsed into the dramatic. Jack's face showed a mixture of emotions; he seemed enthralled when they told of a dead body, and a mixture of frustration and *it's not fair* when he heard of the chase through the tunnels. He put his hands together in a pyramid shape.

'So, you didn't actually kill anyone, and they'll know that when they do their forensic stuff,' Jack announced.

'CSI Post Office eh?' said Wade, not really believing it.

'It's good you made it up and out though.' He smiled.

'Well, it wasn't easy and I've lost a silk scarf!' complained Faiza.

Wade shrugged. 'So, what do we do now then? You're probably just going to tell us to give ourselves up because we're innocent,' he said.

'Well… at first yes – but look, you must have been set up – the free tickets, the snatching from the train, the lies about the knife. You're being framed,' concluded Jack.

'We know that… but why and by who? Who's going to believe *us*?' said Faiza.

'I've an idea – why don't we call Corner and explain it all? She'll know we're being set up,' said Wade enthusiastically.

'What if she's doing the setting up?' countered Faiza.

They sat quietly for a moment.

'Maybe we should find somewhere a little less… public,' said Jack as he looked around.

'For sure, I think we need to think first before we do anything,' said Faiza.

'Yeah definitely,' agreed Jack. 'Need to see what's happening in the real world too. Let's get online.'

I'm getting closer. The man looked at the screens and pointed at two figures leaving the station. The timestamp on the video showed it was recorded about twenty minutes earlier.

'There they are,' he announced. *And they are dressed a little differently too. Howdy, I'm onto you.*

'Which way is that exit?' he asked the CCTV operator.

'Exit Four, towards London Bridge and Southwark Cathedral,' she replied.

'Thanks for the professional courtesy.' *Now I've got you.* He headed out and towards the same exit. As he left, he failed to notice another figure sporting a red baseball cap on the station concourse who seemed to be looking for something or someone.

26

Quickly, quietly, and separately they headed out and east under the road bridge. Maintaining a distance from each other, they travelled down a few roads with Jack taking the lead. Ten minutes later, they found a small café with internet facilities close to the river. Despite mirrored windows, it was a small, slightly grubby place which seemed out of place as part of the ground floor of an old three-storey office block. The building was mostly deserted having been 'sold for redevelopment' some time earlier.

Inside the place it was equally drab – the owner clearly did not believe in paying for electric light. It meant it would be perfect for doing some covert research. The trio ordered some fizzy drinks and bought half an hour online time from a short, stocky man whose badge claimed he was the manager. They chose the computer furthest away from the door.

'Hey, cowboy, don't spill anything on the keyboard,' warned the man as he brought over their fizzy drinks. He headed back behind the counter and through a door marked *Staff Only*.

The man in the long grey coat continued to wander along the roads next to the Thames. *Where are you, where are you?*

'Right let's find out what's going on out there. Wow, what did old people do before the internet?' asked Jack to no-one. Wade nodded and Faiza just rolled her eyes.

'Spare me the nerdy nostalgia, just work out where we go next,' said Faiza impatiently.

Jack logged in and quickly launched a VPN, which, as he explained to Wade, was a way of making sure no-one could track them online. Jack navigated to a news site and all three were dismayed but not surprised that the hunt for them was still underway and they were the topmost trending topic on social media.

'Here, let me,' said Faiza taking the mouse and keyboard. She logged onto a site that you could make anonymous calls from and called home. She was about to hang up after eight rings, when it was answered by Nida, Faiza's mum.

'Faiza, is that you? Are you ok?' came her voice. It sounded tinny and strained through the old computer's speakers.

'Hi, Mum, yes it's me. I—'

'Oh my goodness, Faiza where are you, is Wade with you? We were so worried. They told us you had—' began Nida anxiously.

'I'm ok, we're ok – I found Wade and we're ok and—'

'Faiza, come home. They say you and Wade are involved in something terrible and – just please come home!'

'We didn't do anything, Mum, we had to—' Faiza's explanation was cut off by a man's voice interrupting on the line.

'Miss Saab? This is Inspector Mirabelle and we want you to come home and we'll get all this sorted. All you need to do is—' The line went dead as Faiza hurriedly cut the call.

'Damn. They're at our home too,' Faiza said, closing the

webpage and looking around nervously. 'Mum wants us to come home too.'

'Hey, do you think they're at mine too?' asked Jack mournfully.

Faiza looked at Wade.

'I think they are already, mate – we heard some strange noises, and your dad was… strange. He even apologised to me!' admitted Wade.

Jack blew out his cheeks. 'Well, it's not me that they think murdered someone.' Jack laughed, but he was the only one. 'But someone is setting us all up. So, let's see what Miss Corner says!'

They nodded in agreement and Faiza used the website again to dial the number on Corner's contact card. It rang for what seemed like an age. A tinny voice answered, 'Chief of Operations, Miss Corner's office. Miss Place speaking. Who's speaking please?'

'This is Faiza Saab and…'

'Putting you through now, Miss Saab.' There was a pause with more clicking on the line. Jack imagined groups of people with headphones on pointing at the phone and encouraging Miss Corner to stay on the line longer to trace them, not realising that wouldn't work.

'Corner here,' came the familiar Irish brogue. 'Miss Saab… Faiza, thank heavens you've reached me – how are you and where are you?' Her voice was urgent.

'I'm fine and we're safe, I need to know what's going on.'

'Tell us where you are, and we'll make sure you're safe. I'm presuming you're with your friends. Your families are very worried – we need to get you and take you out of danger.'

'Danger? Look, we didn't do it you know; it wasn't us. I know you told us not to get involved and we didn't, this isn't our fault, we—' gushed Faiza.

'I believe you. Don't panic, but… look someone's after you and we don't think they're going to stop now. Just tell us where you are, and we'll be there within minutes, I promise.'

'How do I know we can trust you? Everyone seems to be after us.'

'We did know where you were, but then you disappeared and we lost track of you. It's so important you trust me and let me get you,' Miss Corner replied.

'How did you know where we were? How do we know we can trust you?' pleaded Faiza.

'There's no time for that now. Look, I've never told you a lie and I'm telling you the truth now – we need to get you to safety. You could be in real danger.'

'Who are the bad guys then and why are they after us? Is it Mr Blue again – has he escaped?'

'No. I can assure you he's still incarcerated and won't be out for a very long time.'

'Can we really trust you?'

'You *need* to trust us,' Corner said after a few seconds. 'Don't trust anyone else, don't just hand yourself in, you *have* to let us come and get you.'

'Why you and not the police?' asked Faiza.

'You need to trust *us* – let us look after you,' repeated Miss Corner. 'Tell us where you are, and we can—'

'We'll be in touch.' Faiza hung up and closed the website. 'That was *not* good.'

'So, she says we're in real danger, but not to just hand ourselves in?' said Wade sceptically.

'Well, I don't feel reassured about that at all either,' mumbled Jack. 'Just who is on our side?'

'Are you sure they can't track us?' asked Wade. Jack shook his head.

'They can't – our location's hidden and—' Jack's

confident reply vanished as all three of them noticed a shadow at the window. Trying to peer through the mirrored window was a man in a long grey coat. As his coat fell open, it could easily be seen that he was carrying a taser.

27

The man entered and quickly scanned the grungy room. The manager came out and looked surprised to see the man was there and that the rest of the place was empty. The man in the coat briefly held up an official-looking ID.

'Oh right... you're quick; I've only just called you. Oh, well, they were here a few moments ago – they must have left,' explained the manager.

The other man looked around again and noticing a recessed door at the back of the room, headed towards it.

'I doubt they went that way – that's just some toilets and a fire escape to the closed offices... You can't—' but his voice was wasted as the man headed through the doorway.

Two floors above, under a desk in a small dark dusty office, Faiza, Wade and Jack sat breathing heavily. They had made a rapid exit from the café into a stairwell and the only way to go was up. The door on the first floor was secured, but the second-floor door was unlocked. It opened into a long corridor with frosted-glass offices and admin spaces off it before opening into a large open-plan office. The lights didn't seem to work, and the place was almost completely dark. So now here they were hiding in the office of a *Mr T Farynor*, the third office along.

'Did you see he had a taser?' hissed Wade.

'Duh yeah, we saw. Do you think he followed us?' asked Faiza.

'I hope not,' whispered Jack.

'Maybe he thinks we went out,' wondered Wade.

Suddenly Faiza put a hand over Wade's mouth, her eyes open wide. From seemingly far away there was a sound of a click – *was that a door closing?* All around them everything was silent, even their breathing.

I know you're up here; I know this is where you are.

Then came a sound. It was hard to hear at first but got louder. Slow footsteps lightly on cheap carpet. They stopped abruptly and there was the sound of a locked office door being rattled. Footsteps again and another door rattle – this time it opened and then shut. Quiet. Whoever or whatever it was had gone into the next office.

Faiza indicated silently that they should go *now*. Quickly and quietly, they left the office. Jack noiselessly closed the door and they tiptoed along into the larger open-plan area. They had somehow sneaked back into the past and it looked like a place where old office machines come to die. Even in the gloom they could make out a place littered with furniture and machines of all sizes and age, but none less than twenty years old. The carpet was a murky brown and threadbare, made worse by the lack of light anywhere – if there were windows, it had been several decades since they had let light in. Wade looked back through the walls of translucent glass and could just make out a shadow moving slowly in the office.

I know this place and I have excellent hearing. I will find you. Let's see if you come out by yourselves…

As they slinked forward into the office graveyard, the noise of the second office unlocking and opening demanded urgency. Faiza dived forward whilst Jack and

Wade headed left and right respectively. They listened and could hear nothing – whoever was there was also being deliberately quiet but that was about to change.

'Wade? Faiza?' came the man's voice, suddenly and loudly breaking the silence. The stunned three were barely even breathing for fear of being heard. 'I'm with the police, and I'm here to take you two into safety. We know you didn't do it, so come on out. It's safe now.' No reply. There was the sound of the door to the third office opening, but it stayed open.

Why aren't they coming out to me? Surely I sound convincing? I know they're here.

A few moments later there came the sound of the office door slamming shut and a voice getting louder as it came closer. 'I know you're in here. I found your hat, Clint Eastwood.'

Wade put his hands on his head and made an anguished face. Neither Jack nor Faiza could see his sorrow but were also making similar faces. Whoever it was knew that they were here and worse, knew *who* they were.

'Come on out, we can talk about it.' No reply.

I am getting sick of this Mr Nice-guy act. Time for action.

'You really should come out – I'll count to three then I'm going to come and find you and I won't be so nice.' He let the words hang there in the air.

Under a desk to the left sat Jack. The desk was surrounded by nothing, just patchy brown carpet, vague furniture shapes and darkness. If the person came this way, there would be no escaping to a better place. He silently pulled the rucksack off his back and pushed himself up against the corner under the desk, pulling out the metal Spitfire and putting it into his pocket. The footsteps he heard were hard to place exactly, with the carpet muffling them and the darkness hiding them. There had to be something he could do. *Think, Jack, think!*

Wade did not move. He could not see past the small machine he had dived behind, but he knew that whoever it was was coming closer. A whispered *three* then a loud clunk with some tinkling on the floor close to him.

Damn them. Now I'll make them regret all of it.

From his position, Wade could just make out the letter *Y* from the typewriter that had been slung to the floor. *Why indeed?* he thought but still did not move and barely breathed. Whoever was hunting them was hoping to frighten someone into moving. *Whoever it was is almost succeeding*, he thought.

'Look, just come out!' came a voice, rudely breaking the silence again. The voice was agitated. There was the sound of something being kicked across the office floor and heavier footsteps getting quieter.

He's going to find me soon enough, Wade thought. Wade peered around the banding machine he was still squeezed next to. Squinting, Wade could just make out a dark shape in front of a blocked-up window. As silently as he could, Wade stepped over the broken typewriter and ducked down by a large black table, dislodging an antique stapler. Like it had something against Wade, the stapler seemed to totter for an age on the edge of the desk. He was too far away to stop it. Then it fell and landed with a thud. In normal circumstances it might have gone unnoticed, but here in this dark, noise-free zone, it was as if the volume had been turned up.

From further up the office, the man turned and thudded his way towards the large black desk. He stopped, breathing heavily.

You must be very close indeed and this is where I get you...

For an age nothing happened, then the man yanked at the desk, pulling it over noisily to reveal… nothing. 'Damn you!' he shouted, kicking the desk once more.

Inside the cupboard next to the now upturned desk, Wade held on to the door hoping the cupboard was invisible. The footfalls were hard to hear but he felt sure he had heard them heading back towards the smaller offices. *How am I going to get out of here and save the others? I can't even see where they are!*

28

It was dark. And still quiet. Jack eased his breathing a little. Had the person gone? Corner's words were still ringing in his mind: *someone is after you and we don't think they're going to stop now.* He had heard the noise of some stationery falling onto the floor and then footsteps heading away. At least the others must be safe. He stopped as he heard the most silent of footsteps. They were coming back.

'I have your sister here,' came the slow voice. 'If you don't come out and join her, things will get even worse for you.' Silence. Darkness.

Wade couldn't leave his sister to face this alone and he was about to come out and admit defeat. He peered out of the crack between the two doors of the cupboard. He could just make out the man in the darkness in the middle of the floor space. Standing next to an upturned desk, he was alone. Wade shrunk down back into the cupboard and nearly yelped as a pencil stabbed him in his behind.

I could wait here all day but I really can't be bothered. The darkness is my friend but it's also yours. Quietly does it...

Jack sat there under the desk and thought. *This person doesn't know I'm here... he thinks it's just Faiza and*

Wade. He's definitely a liar – there's no way Faiza would stay quiet if she was being held. He prayed to himself that the other two were thinking the same as him – *don't trust this person, whoever he is.* There was something familiar about his voice though. It was up to him to save the situation – he would make a run for it through the small offices and the way they had come… at least it would give the others a chance to get away and maybe the man downstairs would help him. *The darkness is helping him, but it's also helping us.*

Wade stood in the cupboard with a pencil partly jammed in his behind wishing he could sit down at least. Maybe he could just run, and the person would chase him freeing the other two, especially as he realised that the person didn't know Jack was here. The worst thing was the silence, punctuated only by the occasional, muted, distant sounds.

What will they do? Maybe it's time I threatened them again.

The voice broke through the silence and their anxious thoughts again, 'I'm going to start throwing things and maybe even using this.' He waved his taser around and lowered his voice. 'So I'm going to count to three. If I get to three, you'll not make it out of here.' He let the words hang in the air and then began his count.
    'One… you know I'm only here to help you.'
    No sounds.
    'Two… this is your last chance, my young friends. This is not a place for kids to hang around looking for trouble.' His words were swallowed up by everything in the darkened room and the silence seemed even more threatening than the man's words. Weeks seemed to pass.

Faiza was closest to the doors but it would still be a clear three seconds across the wispy brown carpet to reach them, during which she would be more than visible. Besides, she couldn't just abandon the other two. She looked frantically around where she was hiding. It was presumably just a cleaner's area with buckets and mops. *What am I going to do?*

A creaking noise broke Jack's thought and not just any creak, it was the creak of shoe leather close by. Jack moved his eyes to the left and nearly shouted out – there by the edge of the desk, not ten centimetres from his face, were two leather shoes. He closed his eyes, wishing it all away. But it wasn't going to just go away. *This man won't stop*, he thought.

Faiza lay in a small, cramped space under a desk close by, feeling angry. It wouldn't have taken much for her to have stood up and thrown everything she had at him. He didn't have her, and she hoped the other two realised that and wouldn't just step out. She moved her foot which was beginning to get pins and needles. As she did so, she scraped the edge of a telephone receiver. The rotary dial fell off and clattered against the edge of the desk with a louder-than-expected clunk.

I know you're by the doors. The shoes creaked as their owner started to walk over towards the noise.

Someone's made a noise, thought Jack. *I have to do something.* He held his breath as the man walked past. Suddenly Jack stood up and shoved the surprised man from behind – hard! The man shouted in anger and surprise but couldn't stop himself tumbling into a tangle of hat stands and old duplicator cables. Jack bolted into the gloom towards the other end of the office, not daring to look back.

Damn you. I can run faster than you and I will get you now!

The man untangled himself and flew into action. Kicking the hat stand, he pivoted on one foot and, with the swish of his coat, ran through the furniture-laden office, vaulting over the last desk.

Where's he gone? The unexpected and sudden sound of a swinging door ahead surprised him. Someone was running downstairs very loudly. *There! There you are – out the far exit.* He pulled at the still-swinging doors and hurtled down the stairway.

As noises of the man faded down the stairs, Jack allowed himself to breathe out slowly, but quietly. He had managed to duck under the last desk before the doors. *Which one of us has escaped?* he thought, peering out from under his desk into the gloom.

Faiza stepped out from behind a hatstand and quickly put a mop through the handles of the double doors, stopping anyone from coming back through them. She walked carefully into the middle of the office area and whispered to join her. Jack looked out and, after peering over the top of the desk, slinked towards where Faiza was. A door opened and Wade came out of the cupboard pulling out a pencil that was lodged in the back of his jeans.

'Phew! Are you okay? Who the hell was that?' asked Faiza.

'I thought he'd gone after you!' exclaimed Wade. 'Who did he run after then?'

'Me...' said Jack a little embarrassed, after a few seconds' silence. 'He started to go towards that noise – Faiza, so I had to stop him'. He nodded towards Faiza and then shrugged. Faiza smiled a little.

'Yeah, I pushed the doors with the mop in the dark and

then threw the bucket down the stairs,' said Faiza quickly. 'He's quick, but not very clever. Jack… Jack, thank you.'

'Brilliant… but we'd better go – the way we came in.' They quickly ran back past the small offices into the stairwell they had come up, just as there was a banging from the doors at the other end of the office.

Damn, they must still be in there – fooled me once but never again. I'm coming back in to get you.

They hurtled down the stairs through the doors back into the tired internet café. From behind the counter, the stocky man looked surprised and stepped backwards. The floor was littered with old PCs and assorted peripherals, and it didn't take much for him to trip and become entangled in it all. Wade and Jack headed for the doors and outside. Faiza stopped and approached the counter, behind which the man lay trying to free himself.

'Hey, greaseball. How did you fall over – were you running away from good taste? If I find you grassed us up and sent that nutcase after us, we're coming back to visit you. And not during the day. *You never saw us.*' She paused and made a deadpan face. 'Stay safe.' And she was gone.

29

They were outside the building in a matter of seconds and rapidly headed away, making every attempt to stay separate. They could hear some police sirens in the distance that seemed to echo around the buildings. Eleven minutes later and they were in a small, recessed garden off a deserted back street next to Shad Thames.

The trio sat breathing heavily on the ground under a closed window, behind a white Kia Sportage that had seen cleaner days.

'Thought we were goners there,' said Jack disjointedly.

'Felt like it, didn't it? We're ok though now, eh?' said Faiza.

'WHO was that and why was he after us? How does he know us?' Jack was trying not to show any anxiousness.

'It's alright, mate; we're ok now,' said Wade comfortingly. 'Jeez, Is *everyone* after us?!'

'I'm a bit scared… I'm not sure what we do next or where we go,' admitted Jack.

'We're all together and we'll do this together,' Faiza announced.

'That bloke's voice seemed familiar… but I can't place it,' replied Jack.

'Like who? Someone in Corner's office? Someone from school?'

'No... ah, it will come to me. I'm sure we've spoken to him before.' Jack frowned. 'But how did he know where we were?' mused Jack to himself.

'Tracking us somehow? Well, it can't be Mr Blue – he's locked up good and proper,' said Wade. 'And Corner said she knew where we were and to trust her!'

'So *she* says,' grumbled Faiza. 'Can we trust her?'

'Corner seems ok to me, maybe we should listen to her?' replied Jack. 'This is all obviously linked to the gold and someone is trying to get us – can't quite work out who or why yet.' Jack's voice trailed off, clearly upset.

Faiza rested her hand on his in a sympathetic gesture. They looked into each other's eyes, briefly, before rapidly pulling their hands apart. Wade looked around him, still on alert.

'Where can we go that's safe?' asked Wade. 'I'm all for getting the hell out of here anyway!'

'Look, we have three choices. We could hand ourselves in to Corner and risk being in worse danger, we could wait here for *Captain Grey* to find us or go on the run for a little longer but to where?' Faiza held her hands out.

They sat for a few silent moments.

'I'm still inclined to believe Miss Corner – she's not a bad person – I vote we head to LPS House and get ourselves protected,' said Jack thoughtfully.

'Protected... or locked away forever in her deepest darkest dungeon. I'm not sure – she's been at the centre of all this. We could just stay on the run for a while?' said Wade wiping the dust off the car with his fingers. He almost liked the idea of being a fugitive.

'Hmm. I'm with the *Calculator Kid*... sorry, I'm with *Jack* here; it's our best chance,' admitted Faiza. 'But maybe to get to Corner in one piece, we'll go there separately and regroup at...'

'Embankment. Yes, Embankment – that's just up the road from LPS House,' cut in Wade.

'Interesting, that's where we thought the rest of the gold might be too!'

'Actually, that's not a bad idea; it's close and people are less likely to see us on the way. Once we're there, we'll work out a way to get to Corner's office,' Jack agreed. 'I'll stick to the south side of the Thames – they'll be less likely to be there.'

'Just stick to as busy an area as possible – and if you're grabbed or threatened, just shout; shout like your life depends on it,' advised Faiza.

'I'll do the Clink and take the long way around,' Wade added as he stood up, followed by Jack and Faiza. They stood motionless for a moment.

'I hope you're not expecting me to hug or give you a motivational speech?' said Faiza a little awkwardly.

'I'd rather hug *Captain Grey*,' replied Wade heading away from the group.

'That can be arranged,' replied Faiza heading in the opposite direction.

'Let's just get there safely,' said Jack and nodded at them both, his eyes locking half a second longer with Faiza. They both looked a little sad, but simply nodded and they were gone. Jack stood for a second, then headed out the way they had come towards the Thames.

None of them noticed a shadow in a long grey coat move away from the window behind them, which was now open. *Patience has never been a virtue of mine, but it looks like it has paid off. I quite like the name Captain Grey... So the rest of the gold might be at Embankment? I think I'll save myself some hassle and meet you there...*

30

In contrast to a previous walking trip that they had made across London, their respective journeys were hassle free – at least to start with. All three kept separate as agreed – Jack headed back along the Thames all the way to Hungerford Bridge. Wade had walked past the Clink and Shakespeare's Globe before heading across Blackfriars Bridge. Faiza, meanwhile, mixed in with tourists crossing London Bridge and then headed up and along part of Bishopsgate.

On any other day they might have sauntered over bridges, stared at the magnificent river and looked at the rich history of the place, soaking up the atmosphere, but today was different. All three of them now had more than enough practice at acting covertly and trying to blend in in plain sight. Faiza had passed Fenchurch Street and the Leadenhall building using all of her now-familiar checking techniques – double-backing, popping in and out of alleyways, heading into shops. She felt pleased with herself by the time she walked up to Embankment Station.

Wade had been tempted to go into the Clink Museum again but kept on heading west. He also did his usual avoidance techniques, like Faiza's. As he no longer had his cowboy hat, he was wearing a tattered old beanie that he had found by Southwark Bridge. He resembled an unfortunate country and western singer, living in colder climes. Sauntering across Blackfriars Bridge, he stopped and watched the river briefly. Two people came and stood next to him, and Wade froze. The couple laughed and looked over the edge. The lady held onto her partner and they walked past Wade. He breathed a sigh of relief and moved on.

Jack's journey was even less eventful as he headed for Hungerford Bridge. Passing the Festival Hall, he could see Embankment Station across the other side. He was sure, after checking multiple times, that no-one was following him. He climbed the metal stairs to bridge level and began crossing. The bridge was busy for a Thursday evening, but he managed to avoid bumping into most of them. A couple with a pushchair stood in the middle of the bridge looking out towards Waterloo Bridge, the lower sun casting a shadow of the bridge onto the fast-flowing water below. Jack stopped and looked over at them, remembering times when he had sat with his great-grandad on the South Bank watching the sun go down.

Jack smiled and looked across at Embankment. He could see Faiza acting nonchalantly by the entrance. He was sure she was about to move on when he saw her look around and then intently at something above the entrance. Then she looked around anxiously and stood to the left of the steps. She was clearly trying to remain inconspicuous whilst keeping a lookout. Jack made a beeline to where he thought Wade might be.

Four minutes later and Jack met Wade by Victoria Embankment Gardens. They pretended not to know each other until they were sure there was no-one watching them, then approached Embankment. People walked in and out of the station and nothing looked amiss – everything looked 'normal'. Inside was a similar picture: ticket machines, tiled floor that had seen better days, people coming up from the Underground and people heading down. No-one paid them any notice at all. They were oblivious to a purple-capped figure sitting in the back of a cab across the road watching them.

Maybe I'll let you find the gold first... then make you pay.

Faiza looked at the people around her, then hurried to the edge of the steps where she spoke in hushed tones.

'I've found something. I know we were going to hand ourselves in to Corner, but I think we should stop and look at this.'

'What?' hissed Wade. 'We're being chased by some maniacs and you want to look at -what, the nice black and white tiles?!'

'Shut up and listen, squib. I think the gold really is here!' whispered Faiza excitedly.

'What... you're starting to sound like me,' said Wade with a big smile.

'There's no need to insult me,' said Faiza in mock anger pointing at the concrete facade. '*Jack*, tell him – it all points to here!'

'She's right,' said Jack continuing to look at the sign and nodding. 'See that inlaid concrete rectangle to the right of the roundel?'

'The roundel? The red roundy thing with a blue Underground sign?' asked Wade.

'Right... well, look what's faintly inscribed into it,' continued Jack.

Wade squinted.

'That backwards C motif!' cut in Faiza. Earlier when they had been frantically looking for clues, they had noticed that some of those involved had sported a ring with a backwards *C*. And now here it was again. They stood for a few seconds despite being tutted at by people trying to get past. Faiza smiled a *look what I found* smile.

'But that means… that means.. it could be here!' Wade became much more animated. 'Well let's go in, let's go in!'

'Hang on, are you seriously suggesting we pop down there and have a looksee? After all we've been through and considering all of TFL, the BTP, CO8 and just about anyone else you can name with a strange acronym is after us?' Jack's voice faded away. He was beginning to realise that he too was excited by the idea of another clue.

There was a pause. Faiza raised her eyebrows, possibly at Jack saying so much.

'Well, we have two options then,' explained Faiza. 'We can hope that Corner is on the level and safe and we don't get done over before we find her. Or we can pop down here and go to ground until it's safe again. Can you think of a better place to go and hide away?'

'Oh and maybe follow the trail for the bullion whilst we're down there!' said Wade loudly.

They looked at each other as Faiza put her thumb up followed by Wade. They looked at Jack who made a face like a fly had flown into his mouth. His thumb went up after a few seconds and they headed in across the black and white tiles towards the barrier gates.

Gotcha.

31

Faiza was first through the barriers. Faced with a range of lines and platforms in front of them, they both looked at Jack. He shrugged.

'So that code – *CC NL 09 126s* – must indicate the Northern Line. Interesting that's where most of our solutions seem to lie recently,' said Jack.

'And problems,' quipped Faiza.

They had no idea what they would find as they headed quickly down the escalator; Wade still half-expected to find a crate of gold in a corner somewhere. They reached the bottom of the moving staircase and headed to the platform, where they found... nothing.

Like the ticket hall above, the scene on the southbound Northern Line platform looked completely normal. A few people – in pairs and in groups – lined the platform, some close to the edge, some further away. The train indicator board showed that the next train was due in two minutes to *Kennington via CX*, whatever that meant. There was some hoarding at the southern end of the platform, but that kind of thing was on every tube station on every line.

'Well, where is it? Any clues at all?' asked Wade, increasingly exasperated as they walked the full length of the platform.

Jack shrugged his shoulders. 'I think we should keep an eye out for that motif… it might still be here somewhere,' he said to no-one in particular.

All three of them walked to the far end, then back to the southern end. A train came in and lots of people got on and off. They tried to act nonchalantly as people walked about them. The doors closed and, with a gust of air, the train left into the void towards Waterloo.

Breathing a sigh of relief, Wade's gaze rested on the hoarding to the left. There were the obligatory notices about *authorised persons only* and there was *no access without talking to the station controller*. But there was no padlock on the door. Without mentioning it, Wade twisted the handle and gasped as he found it opened. He pushed Faiza in front of him and quickly pulled Jack, who was still looking at where the train had just gone, after him and closed the wooden door.

'What are you doing?' protested Jack and Faiza together.

'I think we're onto something,' Wade whispered.

'On the right track then?' Jack mused.

'Yes, we're going off the rails,' chipped in Wade.

'Shut up, both of you – what have you found?' The area they were in was only about two metres long. It had all the usual items you might expect to find behind workmen's hoardings: some cones, yellow and red tape, two shovels, some hardhats, blackened cables of various length. At the far end where the hoarding ended and behind some large metal poles, the old wall was exposed. Faiza pulled at the clips to show more of the wall. At the bottom of this part of the blackened wall was a similarly black piece of iron, about half a metre square. Scratched into one corner of it was the familiar backwards *C* motif.

Wade hopped over to it and pulled at the metal. It took

a few attempts but eventually it opened. He was about to duck through when Jack held onto his arm.

'Are you sure? I… this feels like we're just climbing into a T-Rex's cave,' Jack said.

Wade grinned and ducked through.

'Looks like a good place to hide from whoever is after us… and Corner!' whispered Faiza as she peered in. 'Come on, Jack, let's do this together.'

Jack looked doubtful but then nodded. 'Ladies first,' he said and smiled.

She gave him an odd look before tentatively following Wade through. Jack looked around him sadly and, realising he was on his own, followed the other two.

'This doesn't feel good!' he whispered as he looked around him. They were in a small two-metre-wide tunnel which disappeared into darkness. The plate swung shut behind them and it suddenly got a lot darker. There was a rank smell and the sound of water somewhere. Some kind of scuttling sound came from up ahead in the darkness. Jack switched on his phone light which made the pale, familiar jagged light patterns, having been partially broken the previous week.

'It's ok – it's on permanent airplane mode since Wade almost destroyed it last week,' he said as he saw the worried look in Faiza's eyes. The floor was dusty and looked damp.

'Hang on, that code said 126… so if that was steps, then we need to start counting and head 126 steps along,' said Faiza. 'I'll count.'

Less than halfway along the small tunnel and already there were drips of water and puddles in the semi-gloom. They couldn't see much, but they could certainly see pools of oily water and rodents scuttling past them.

'Why is it always darkness, rats and water?' mumbled Jack, trying hard to follow Wade.

'It's alright for you – this is the second time today I've been underground!' moaned Wade.

'That's 'cos you didn't invite me!' replied Jack.

'It was my dad's family invitation – I wish you'd been there,' admitted Wade.

'Then you wouldn't have got blamed for murder?'

'Then I could have blamed you for it.'

'Nah, you look the type, I don't.'

'Ha ha. It must have been a set-up,' concluded Wade.

'Duh, do you think?' said Jack sarcastically.

'Seventy-two steps… It's like *The Chuckle Brothers – The Next Generation* – seventy-five steps,' sighed Faiza as they carefully walked forward.

Wade reached out to steady himself on the wall but took his hand away quickly. The rough wall was slimy, cold, and reminded him of a snake's skin.

'We're never going to find this gold are we?' said Wade. 'Every time we get closer, we seem to take a step back or get chased by some mad person.'

'I think we've done amazing things so far, for pesky kids!' Faiza laughed. 'And we did find most of it already!'

'Yeah come on, we're still all in it together,' added Jack.

'Hmm, I'm still not hopeful we'll *ever* find it,' Wade sighed.

'Ugh, what's that?' said Wade a minute later as Faiza made 120. Jack shone the light up and it lit up a white bricked wall. Inset into it was a large black metal door behind a large metal gate. Above it was a sign that read, *Watertight doors must be kept closed at all times*, with a number for the inspection engineer. Wade tapped the door through the bars – it had heavy condensation on it, and it felt solid, as though there was some heavy weight behind it.

'That's a mighty strong door and it's very cold,' Wade said pulling his hand away.

'I don't reckon we should try and go through that one,' said Jack.

'Duh, do you think?' quipped Wade.

Jack tried to smile in the semi-darkness and shone his fractured light down to the left of the gate.

'Hey look,' Wade spluttered, his voice low. 'Now that *does* look familiar.'

Jack bent down and looked closer at what Wade had seen. Jack smiled and tentatively put his hand on a set of ceramic tiles at floor level. They were grimy and obscured by dust, but there in amongst the white and grey tiles were ten, small, tarnished brass plates, in two rows of five. Stretching down, Jack pulled at the closest of the brass plates with his fingers. It came away easily, helped by decades of deterioration, and clattered lightly onto the floor. Behind it was the almost expected old-fashioned electrical socket. It was like a modern socket, but the holes were larger and rounder.

'That's like those old sockets we saw at Bank that opened the hidden doorway!' exclaimed Wade growing more excited.

Jack nodded. 'And look – the letters and numbers we saw too,' he observed. Previously, at Bank station, they had used a code to work out the location of a socket that opened a hidden doorway.

'Looks like we've found old Plum's handiwork again… this must be the same thing,' added Faiza. 'Ugh, but look, there's ten sockets this time – how do we know the right one?'

They all recalled how Jack had been electrocuted. They stood quietly for a few moments, the only sounds were dripping and scuttling.

'Well, you're used to this, Jack – just try a few of them. Come on, Jack, have a go again,' enthused Wade.

Jack and Faiza shook their heads.

'Hang on – he's not sticking his fingers in those sockets! Last time he got a big shock – it could be any one of them!' exclaimed Faiza defiantly.

'Well, how will we know? One of them must be the right one!' said Wade exasperated.

'Yes but why don't *you* stick your fingers in there then?' argued Faiza. 'Which one do you think it is, Jack?'

'Well, if I were to hazard a guess, I'd say we already know,' said Jack confidently. Without another word, from his rucksack, he pulled out the increasingly mangled toy Spitfire, pulled one of the plates off and put the wing into the socket.

32

Wade and Faiza took a step back and Faiza gasped. Nothing. No fizz, no sparks and definitely no electricity.

'What are you doing? That could have been dangerous!' spluttered Faiza, pushing him.

'Nicely done, Jack.' Wade smiled and patted his friend on the back, but he showed he was more than a little relieved.

Jack quietly breathed a sigh of relief too. 'I chose socket number nine because—' began Jack.

'Yes – that was the number on that sequence we had!' cut in Faiza remembering the code they had unearthed: CC *NL 09 126S*. 'Nicely done… but be careful, eh?' She pushed him lightly again.

In the darkness, no-one saw Jack blush.

'So what did it do…?' Wade asked looking around. 'Try it again.'

Jack turned the metal in the socket again and further away, above the sound of drips and scuttling, came a light click. Jack slid the plane back into his pocket.

Listening intently, and without a word, they walked back along to where the sound of the click had come from – about thirty steps further back on the left-hand side.

There was also a quiet clump from the entrance, but that could have been anything including the myriad of creatures and other things that seemed to find their way into these tunnels.

'Here,' said Wade, feeling the grimy wall with his hands. 'This feels like the edge of something.'

Faiza felt where Wade had hold of and together they pulled. A hinged piece of wood designed to look like the wall opened about half a metre wide. All three of them stood there in stunned silence for a moment before Wade slid through.

'Honestly, what is it with you two today? Just rushing into things!' Faiza tutted.

'Oh you'd have pushed me through anyway!' came Wade's voice.

'Actually you're right, I'm glad you went first. You ok? What can you see?'

'I'm in a small tunnel, which I think leads to another one – come on through.' Wade pushed the door open a little more.

Faiza smiled at Jack which he took as his 'invite' to go next. Faiza followed and the door closed behind them with a soft click.

The door led into a much smaller musty tunnel that they had to duck down in. At the other end of the five-metre-long passageway was another sheet of metal which wasn't attached. It was very dark and the fractured light on Jack's phone was fading.

'My phone's almost out of battery – should we keep going forward?' said Jack, squinting in the darkness.

'Either that or we head back into the real world,' sighed Faiza.

'Forward of course!' said Wade.

The other two nodded.

'What do you think is behind the door?' asked Jack.

'No idea, but we're going through it… ready?' Wade whispered.

'Why are you whispering? I would imagine the world knows we are coming now!' Jack said back.

Wade ignored him. 'Here we go! Let's make an entrance!' he said, still in a whisper. Before they had a chance to react, Wade shouted a 'Rahhhhhhhhh!' as they rushed through the doorway.

As Wade's shout echoed into nothingness, they could see that the small doorway opened into a large cylindrical shaft, about thirty metres high. They were on one of several metal walkways that criss-crossed the shaft at different levels and the one they were on was about ten metres up from the darkness. They couldn't see what was below them, just an absence of light, but they could feel a strong downdraft of air. They all looked up to where the light was coming from. Some fifteen metres above them in the ceiling were two large slowly rotating fans and a pale, yellow light.

'Maybe you scared them away with your roar?' sniggered Faiza.

'Wow, where are we?' asked Wade, ignoring her and looking around.

'Probably some long-forgotten ventilation shaft,' replied Jack nonchalantly. 'Not sure what's beneath us, but I wouldn't like to go down there.'

'I'm more interested in what *that* is,' said Faiza pointing to the top walkway. At the end of it, closer to the light, was a rusty metal plate inset into the wall at ankle level. It looked like it didn't belong there.

'Let's go look – me first!' Wade forged ahead to the end of the walkway they were on and through a door-sized recess. 'Come on!'

The others followed. In the recess was a thin spiral staircase. They followed it up past two other walkways and onto the top one. They could see it more clearly now; it had a rusty handle next to some dusty brass discs and a dial marked with *Yale* and was clearly very old. Wade sat determinedly in front of it. The metal walkway gave a moan and seemed to sigh as the other two joined him.

'It's a safe,' Wade said matter-of-factly.

Faiza rolled her eyes and reached down to pull at the handle but, as expected, it did not open. Wade tried pulling it and Jack even had a go.

'Well what's the combination then?' asked Wade looking at Jack.

'No idea… but look, there must be a way to work out the combination. Think back, what do we know? What have we seen already that could help,' said Jack. 'Maybe those things we saw on the USB?'

They sat for a minute and tried to remember. Jack was about to get his ailing phone out to find the photos of the documents when there came the click of fingers.

'Hang on a minute,' said Faiza, suddenly wide-eyed, 'remember that long sentence with directions…?' There was a pause as the other two remembered what Faiza was talking about.

'Yes!' Jack burst into life. 'That's it – it's not directions, it's the combination!'

'Yeah… me and you make a good team eh, Jack?' She beamed.

'Yes, we *all* do!' came a slightly disgruntled Wade. 'So what did it say?'

Jack shook his phone and the light grew a little stronger for a second. He quickly scrambled through the photos on his phone.

'Still no signal… battery is at 3%,' he mumbled as he

pressed on various bits of his screen. 'Yes, here it is… go right twice stop at a turn left once past a stop at b turn right stop at c.' His voice trailed off as he thought about it.

'So what is *a* then?' asked Wade. 'And *b* and *c*?'

'Could it be the numbers we saw already… the *126* and the *9*?' asked Faiza.

'Might be… hang on, what about that other sheet with the time on it?' said Wade.

'I was just thinking that – It said eight fifty-five so let's try 8-5-5 for ABC,' said Jack.

'See, WE make a good team eh, Jack?' said Wade a little smugly as Faiza raised one eyebrow.

Jack followed the instructions; he turned it twice to the right and stopped at eight, then turned it left back past eight and stopped at five before turning it back to the right stopping at five. He stopped. Silence again as he pulled on the handle. Nothing. It didn't budge, just squeaked a little.

'Try it again, try it again!' Wade insisted.

Jack did so, but the result was the same. They felt dejected as they sat around the locked plate wondering what to do next. Jack tapped his fingers on the safe and looked intently at it.

'Why would he note down the wrong numbers for the combination?' said Wade, breaking the silence.

'Plum would have hidden it in plain view,' announced Faiza thoughtfully. 'You know what he was like.'

'Maybe it should be c then b then a?' asked Wade.

Jack frowned and tried it anyway, but, as he expected, they got the same result. Just a squeaky handle.

'Faiza is right… he would have made it easy for him, but no-one else,' said Jack smiling at Faiza in the darkness. 'So eight fifty-five… eight fifty-five…' he said out loud a few times. Suddenly he laughed which took them both by surprise.

'What, what, what is it, Jack?' asked Wade a little shocked.

Jack laughed a little more and shook his head. 'It's eight fifty-five... eight fifty-five!' he announced. The others look perplexed. 'Eight fifty-five... five to nine... FIVE TWO NINE!'

Wade and Faiza sat there open-mouthed and then nodded. They encouraged him to try the new numbers. Jack repeated the instructions on the safe, but this time used five for a, two for b and nine for c. He put his hand on the handle.

'I want us all to do this,' he said quietly.

The other two nodded and Faiza put her hand on Jack's.

'This still doesn't mean we're married... yet!' said Faiza laughing.

Jack turned a shade of red as Wade tutted and put his hand on Faiza's.

'Right. Let's count to three,' said Jack. 'Ready... one... two...'

'Hang on!' said Wade. 'Do we go on three or after three?'

'THREE!' shouted Faiza impatiently and together they pulled the handle. The safe door creaked open. They gasped.

Laughter echoed off the walls of the ventilation shaft. Lots of small bars of gold seemed to be trying to spill out of the safe. They had found the bullion and, even in the semi-light, it shone. The three laughed some more as each of them held up a bar. Faiza hugged Wade and then hugged Jack. Wade and Jack slapped each other's shoulders. They had done it; the gold had been found. They weren't going to count it here, but there were over seventy bars at least!

The light in the shaft was poor but reflected brightly off the gold and for a while it made everything seem fabulous again. Their revelry was cut short, however, by the walkway creaking and a person's shadow falling across the bullion.

33

'Hello, hooligans,' came the voice from behind them.

The three stopped their gold-handling celebrations and looked around. Behind them stood a man in an orange Hi-Viz jacket and purple cap. He had the pale yellow light behind him so they couldn't quite make out his face but could see he was holding a taser.

'Who… what, who are you?' spluttered Wade shuffling back as far as he could.

The man laughed. Faiza started to get up, but the man raised a hand.

'Just stay very still, all of you. So we meet at last. You've led me a merry dance and cost me so much time! I wonder if you saw this coming or whether this is like *Scooby doo* and you all gasp as I reveal who I am,' said the man, ignoring Wade. A sinister silence hung in the air as the smug man appeared to milk every second of this.

He was about to speak again when Jack spoke. 'You are Mr Tim – that miserable Underground assistant in the Hi-Viz vest we met at Bank,' said Jack matter-of-factly and more bravely than he felt.

'You mean miserable Station *Manager!* I remember you, Jack,' said the man stepping more into what little there was of the light. 'The quiet, clever one.'

'Mr Tim...?' quizzed Wade. '*Mr Tim*? What, you're that bloke who stupidly chased us around the Underground?'

'And you're Wade, the more-brawn-than-brains type. And this is Faiza again too. Yes, I remember you all from when we met at Bank. And more recently too. Wow, I had a lot of fun secretly watching you over the last few weeks. You were lucky on that school trip.'

'You... you nearly killed us on that ride at the adventure park!' said Jack angrily, remembering back to their recent school trip to the Risa Land of Adventures.

'Well, I only meant to maim or seriously harm you, so that's ok,' he said with a sneer.

'Why, what did we ever do to you?!' complained Wade loudly.

'You three cheated me and my brother out of our golden birthright and managed to get him locked up so now I'm making you pay. It's very simple.'

'Your brother – what? Who's locked up?' asked Wade.

'Haven't you worked it out yet, cowboy? Haven't you realised who my brother is? You guys really are thick, eh?' He said the last sentence slowly to all of them as though he was talking to three-year-olds.

'Oh no, you mean *Mr Blue*? You're related to Plum?' said Faiza disbelievingly. They sat in silence for a few seconds as the new information washed over them.

'Wow, the penny drops, a bit like the rest of you in a few minutes, if you don't do exactly as I say.'

'You're really related to Plum?' Wade repeated.

'Tadahh! It's me.' He made jazz hands. 'Me and my brother, we realised at an early age that Grandad Plum had hidden a fortune in gold and just as we were getting close, you lot came along and stole it from us!'

All three of them tried to stifle a giggle at the mention of a *Grandad Plum*.

'You mean we recovered the gold that *he* had stolen,' chipped in Jack.

'I had the perfect job to track it down... and I was almost there!' he continued. 'So I made it my business to make you all pay. I had no idea you'd be able to find the rest of Corner's Calamity, so yes, you can call me *Captain Grey* or Mr Tim. I've got lots of names.'

I bet you do, thought Wade.

'I set up the Post Office tickets and arranged a murder charge – I even tracked you to that old building thanks to a tracker in your jacket and a good bit of detective work, but still you managed to slide out of reach. Well not any-more.' He looked back at Faiza again, who just stared back at him. If looks could kill.

'So you just, what – made it your mission to follow us about like a sad, cross puppy?' said Faiza screwing her face up.

Mr Tim was about to argue back but instead just shook his head. 'Right, enough trips down memory lane.'

'What... what are you going to do?' asked Jack in a voice without confidence.

'Well, duh – I'll be relieving you of all this wonderful gold, before leaving you trapped in here. Or worse.'

'You can't take our gold!' protested Wade.

Mr Tim looked around the shaft mockingly. 'Hmm, looks like I can. First... you three stand up slow... that's right.' He aimed the taser at them and they slowly stood up. 'Now head back down the stairs to the middle walk-way... hands in the air, one at a time!' As he shuffled from one foot to another, the walkway groaned a little as though the metal was tired. 'Go on – one at a time. Jovial Jack, you go first, and leave your bag eh.'

He waved the taser at them and Jack slowly dropped his rucksack on the floor in front of the safe. Looking at the other two and realising he had no choice, Jack backed down the stairway. On the way down, he pulled the remains of his Spitfire from his pocket and left it on the bottom stair. He emerged with hands again in the air. Mr Tim, meanwhile, began putting the gold bars into the rucksack. He looked through the metal grid of the walkway and indicated that Jack should go to the middle of the lower walkway before pointing the taser at Faiza.

'Don't try anything or your rootin'-tootin' brother here buys it.' Mr Tim was waving the taser around like a conductor's baton.

Faiza looked at Wade who nodded and she too backed slowly down the stairs briefly out of sight. She almost tripped on the metal plane. She picked it up and slid it into her hair band.

Mr Tim watched her emerge and nodded. 'Your turn, hooligan number three,' he said with a grin.

Wade looked at the other two on the lower walkway and headed down.

'Now don't y'all move now,' he said in a sing-song voice. 'This little 'lectric thing will electrify you and the whole of that metal walkway so don't move a muscle.' Keeping one eye on the lower walkway, he filled the rest of the bag, scooping up the gold from the safe. He rolled the rucksack onto his back and stood up slowly. 'Woah, that's heavy.' He swayed backwards a little but put out a hand to steady himself.

'You can't get away,' Wade shouted up, 'and Corner's heavies will be here soon.'

'No, they won't. CO8 think you're responsible for a murder. I do hope that Corner is out of a job soon. I got my journalist friend *Dudman* to really lay it on thick, but then somehow you got that Miss Corner to whisk you away!'

'We didn't call her,' protested Wade.

Mr Tim looked like he was about to shout something but shook his head instead. 'Enough now. Well, I guess it's time you all went for a swim…'

34

'It's *plain* that you're a bit mad,' said Jack suddenly out of nowhere.

Faiza turned to look at him wide-eyed but nodded as she understood the reference. Wade looked at him with a puzzled expression.

'That's not nice, Jack,' Mr Tim said, pointing the taser right at him, 'and I thought you were the nice, quiet one!'

Suddenly Faiza reached into her hair and whipped the metal plane out, throwing it through the semi-darkness at Mr Tim.

'Well, I hope you can all swim because—' Mr Tim didn't finish his sentence. The metal Spitfire clanged against the handrail, hit the wall and landed a few metres behind him. He turned rapidly and almost overbalanced, again holding onto the handrail. This time the whole walkway made a louder metallic groan and seemed to drop a few centimetres. Two of the four bolts holding the metal walkway had sheared off.

Mr Tim gripped even tighter and shouted, 'You missed! I was going to just leave you here, but now I'm really going to—' He stopped mid-threat as two of the gold bars fell from his rucksack and clattered onto the walkway. Mr Tim looked at them, then at the gold and back to them again. He tried to shift his weight to get closer to the dropped gold bars. At that moment, the end of the walkway creaked a little more. The bolt holding it snapped and the walkway dropped half a metre. Mr Tim lurched forward and bent over causing the rucksack – laden with over seventy small bars of wartime gold – to slide over his head.

The instinct of greed grabbed Mr Tim before he had time to even think about it and he reached out to catch the bag. As he did so, he let go of the handrail and just managed to grab the rucksack as it slid towards the edge of the walkway. Fortunes had changed; Faiza, Wade and Jack were safe some fifteen metres below as Mr Tim struggled above.

'Let go of the gold and you can climb back up!' shouted Wade.

'I'm not falling for that,' Mr Tim grunted. 'Don't move or… or I'll—'

'You'll throw gold at us?' snapped Faiza. 'Come on just let it go, it's pulling the walkway down!'

The walkway groaned again and the end suddenly dropped another half metre. Mr Tim watched the taser slip out of his grasp. The taser whizzed past them and hit the lowest walkway. A few of the bars tumbled out of the rucksack that Mr Tim was grasping and disappeared off the walkway and into the darkness with a splash. No doubting now – there was a lot of water beneath them. The upper walkway was now facing downwards at forty degrees and Mr Tim was struggling to keep both himself and what was left of the gold-filled rucksack from plunging.

'Can't we do anything?' asked Wade, looking at Jack.

Jack was about to reply, when Faiza pushed past them.

'Wait here. I mean it, stay here.' She ran forward and dis-appeared into the stairway.

Wade went to move forward too, but Jack held onto him. 'Don't, Wadey – you heard her,' he said urgently. 'Too many up there would make it worse.'

'But I can't… she can't just…' Wade's voiced trailed off as he saw Faiza's silhouette at the top of the shaft.

Fifteen metres above them, Faiza appeared on the top level. The distance between the edge of the wall where the safe was and the end of the walkway was about a metre down. Looking across to the other end of the walkway, Faiza could see that the last two bolts holding it were straining and bending. Mr Tim had one hand on the edge of the metal and his other hand holding onto the heavy rucksack.

'Give me your hand!' she shouted.

'No you want my gold, you'll take my gold,' he shouted back.

'Forget that, most of it's safe on the walkway. Just grab my hand and I'll pull you up!' Faiza was determined and reached out to him, but he refused to let go of his prize. There was a snapping sound as one of the two remaining bolts gave way and the walkway dropped another few centimetres. Mr Tim began to slide forward and scrambled in vain to stop his slide towards the drop. Finally he let go of the metal and reached out towards Faiza.

From where they were, the boys could only see shapes against the pale light. There was clattering and the sound of metal on metal. There was some shouting and the walkway juddered. Jack squinted in the increasing dark-ness. *What is Faiza doing up there?*

'Oh come on, we have to do something now!' shouted Wade at Jack. They moved forward a step, but, before they could figure out what, something fell, hit the walkway above them with a clank and whooshed past them. A second later, from the darkness below, came the sound of two loud splashes.

35

Wade and Jack stared down into the darkness and didn't breathe. There was no more splashing, just the distant sound of water lapping around the edges. Wade looked up to see… no-one. The walkway swayed gently in the dust and pale light. There was no-one up there.

'Faiza, Faiza?!' Wade and Jack both shouted, looking down again into the abyss. Their voices echoed off the stone walls, but silence was the only reply. Wade went to climb the side of the walkway, but Jack held him back.

'It's no use, mate, you'll drown too!' he shouted.

'I can't just leave her – she's my sister!' Wade struggled.

'Oh, let him jump,' came a voice from the doorway. 'It means I can have his bedroom.'

They spun round to see Faiza standing there. She looked a little dusty, but she was there, and she was alive.

'Ah you almost look pleased to see me!' she said with a hint of mirth.

They stood in front of each other and hugged.

'Oh my days, I am SO glad you're ok… you scared us rushing off like that!'

'Oh no, do you think I'm turning into you?' Faiza made a mock horrified face.

'I'm glad you're ok too,' came Jack's slightly quieter voice as the events of the last few minutes caught up with him. 'I'm… glad you're ok.'

Faiza smiled and put a hand on his shoulder. They all looked over the edge. There was not a sound. If they hadn't heard the splashes, they wouldn't even have known there was water there.

'Is he gone?' asked Wade, after a few moments. Still nothing from the abyss.

'I think so… what happened up there?' asked Jack, looking back up.

'I tried to get him to take my hand… I tried. He just wouldn't let go of the gold.' Faiza looked sadly down at the water.

'Do you think he's…?' said Wade without finishing the sentence.

They looked again down at the darkness. Nothing.

'Did the rucksack go in too?' asked Jack, frowning. The others looked around and down but could make out nothing. 'Oh no – my plane's probably gone forever too!'

'Yeah, what *was* that about being *plain*?' asked Wade.

'*Plane* – I thought the best bet was to create a diversion, so I left the plane on the bottom step in the few seconds that I was out of sight.'

'Nice throw too, Faiza,' said Jack, nodding.

'Well, nice throw for a girl,' added Wade, laughing.

Faiza stared at him.

'No… no… no way, I didn't mean that! I meant you throw like a boy.' Wade laughed.

'You'd better be joking, squib!' She pushed him. The walkway they were on made a light creaking noise.

'I don't like it here. Let's get out before the rest of it comes down,' said Jack, heading off the walkway and back to the smaller tunnel. They emerged back into the main tunnel and turned left towards the way they had come in. They made sure the door did not close completely in case they had to get back in.

'I think we should just go straight to Corner and CO8 now,' said Faiza. The other two nodded in agreement. It was ninety-six steps but they stopped in their tracks after just sixty. Someone was coming through the small iron door from the main platform. Although it was dark, there was nowhere to hide. Whoever it was pushed his way through the opening and stood there staring right at them. Because of the poor light, all they could see was the silhouette of a large man.

'Miss Saab, Mr Roble and Mr Carter? Is that you?' The voice was familiar but welcome.

'Mr Ruby?!' All three of them were stunned. He smiled that disarming smile – even visible in the gloom – and held up a welcoming hand.

'Yes, 'fraid so. I'm part of CO8.' He held up his ID. 'Look, let's save the introductions and explanations till later – tell me in short order what's happened.'

'It was Tim Plum!' spluttered Jack.

'He tried to kill us!' added Wade. 'With a taser!'

'Where is he now?' Mr Ruby said seriously, looking past them into the darkness.

'He fell off the walkway into that flooded shaft back there,' said Faiza, urgently pointing further back along the tunnel. 'There's a rucksack full of gold too!'

'Do you think he made it out?' Ruby asked walking a few metres past them and then back.

'I don't think so... it's a long way to the bottom of the shaft,' Jack said sadly.

'Mr Ruby? Seriously?' said Wade disbelievingly.

Ruby ignored him. 'We should be ok, but Plum could still be around. Come on.' Mr Ruby walked ahead of them towards where he had come in. 'Stay close and do exactly as I say. By the way, nice outfit, Wade,' he said, smiling.

Wade just frowned.

'And the worst thing is that I lost my rucksack and model Spitfire,' Jack said suddenly. 'That's helped us all the way,' he added wistfully.

'Your own little sonic screwdriver, eh?' added Faiza.

Jack and Wade looked at her in admiration.

'Geek,' she added, smiling.

They emerged back into the area surrounded by hoarding to find the hoarding had gone. In front of them stood seven large figures in black combat fatigues, all with rather large guns pointing at them. There was suddenly a lot of shouting and orders to 'lie on the floor', which the three did extremely quickly and without any further prompting. Mr Ruby held his ID up and it immediately went silent, and Wade wondered if he had been struck deaf. One of the figures stepped forward and lifted his balaclava.

'It's ok, it's them. Weapons low. Sit rep, now,' the man said authoritatively to Mr Ruby. Jack recognised his face as Agent Three-Seven, Miss Corner's right-hand man.

'Three civilians saved. Suspect has disappeared into the water in the disused shaft. Should be considered extremely dangerous.'

Jack and Wade nodded furiously.

'You two,' Ruby said, pointing at two of the operatives, 'get them out of here, gently, to LPS House. No need for isolation protocol. The rest of you follow me.'

Without another word they were led away along the now deserted platform. Their last view before leaving the platform was of Mr Ruby and the remaining five men heading through the door.

The whole station was deserted having been placed into

a large-scale lockdown. This contrasted with the hordes of people lining the pavements as they headed up and out of the station. Jack counted seven police cars, five vans – some blacked out – and two black cars. The three were bundled into one of the two black cars and it sped away with sirens blaring.

'Are you ok, all of you?' the voice of Miss Place, Miss Corner's assistant, came over the car intercom.

All three of them answered that they were fine.

'Glad you're safe. I'll admit it's been hard keeping track of you. We're going to debrief you in our discussion suite first, those are the orders,' she said authoritatively and then clicked off.

'Debrief? Ugh, here we go again then, bet its Suite Number Four,' sighed Wade trying to peer out.

'Blimey, Ruby was one of theirs? Did you know Ruby was their agent?' Faiza asked Jack.

'Well it wasn't obvious but, well, sort of, he gave some clues. So yes, but, well, kind of…'

'Ha ha, basically not then,' Wade laughed. 'He really didn't seem the type.'

'How did Ruby know we were there?' asked Faiza. 'Did he follow us?'

'I think Mr Ruby has had his eye on us for a long time,' replied Jack thoughtfully. 'Him and that Mr Tim.'

'So, he was after us because of what we did to his miserable brother, Mr Blue? If only he'd have waited a few minutes, he could have tried to take the gold in the tunnel,' said Faiza.

'He comes from a greedy family,' remarked Jack.

'It's kind of ironic how Mr Tim almost came to the same end as me and Jack at the funfair – stuck up high on something metal that was giving way,' said Wade.

'Wow, yeah… I'm amazed actually,' said Faiza.

'At what?'

'That you know a word like ironic. That's about three new words in the last week!'

They laughed as the world whizzed by.

'Time to face the music then, I guess. If she starts having a go, then I'll give her hell – this time it wasn't our fault,' argued Faiza.

'I don't know, I think she'll just be glad to see us,' said Jack quietly.

They approached a dull brown warehouse door that looked like it had not been opened for years. As the car slowed, the driver pressed a button on his steering wheel. The door slid quickly open and closed again as they zipped inside. The difference in environments didn't surprise them as they had been there several times before, but usually they didn't use this entrance.

They entered the smart-looking shiny lift. Wade pointed at the wall panel which showed a few further lower floors than the one they had got in at. All three of them smiled, remembering their own experiences in the firing range in the bowels of LPS House. The lift moved quickly up to the fourth floor, and they were ushered along the corridor into the now-familiar Discussion Suite Four.

36

Miss Corner sat at the head of the large wooden table which was festooned with drinks and food again. She smiled broadly and got up to greet them as they came in with Agent Four-Five. She shook the hands of Wade and Jack, and hugged Faiza. They were a little wary of her at first – this seemed to be a different type of Miss Corner.

'Firstly, are you sure you're all ok?' she began.

They nodded.

'Do let us know if you need anything,' she continued, ushering them all to sit down.

They sat down and all of them began talking at once. Miss Corner raised her hand and the cacophony of voices stopped.

'Let's do this one at a time.' She shuffled some papers. 'Help yourselves to the refreshments and I'll start; we have informed your families you are safe and that we will be bringing you home shortly. They are very relieved after the terrible things they heard and read today – they, and we, do understand that this wasn't entirely your doing and that you have come through quite an ordeal.'

Faiza, Wade and Jack all breathed a sigh of relief.

'Hang on,' interrupted Faiza, '*none* of it was our fault – being chased by a madman, accused of doing away with some bloke!'

'Right, well, we'll get to the bottom of it, but please let me continue,' replied Miss Corner putting her glasses back on.

Faiza remained stony faced.

'Secondly, we are, I am, so happy you are safe and well. Before we begin a debrief, it does appear that we owe you an apology. We were not fast enough; we were not good enough to prevent this and we should have been.' She looked at the confusion on their faces. 'The information we received was incomplete and as a result you were left in more danger than you should have been. I am deeply sorry for that.'

'Ah don't worry yourself, Miss Corner,' cut in Wade. 'It was fun.' He beamed whilst munching into a cream puff. The other two looked at him, mouths open. 'Well, it *was* fun. Mostly.'

Corner continued, 'Thank you, cowboy.' She smiled briefly before continuing, 'First, I need to hear from you exactly what happened. Miss Saab, you seem to be the most vocally coherent of your little gang, would you like to start – from when I last saw you?' Faiza smiled as both Jack and Wade frowned. 'You two can chip in when you feel the need.'

Faiza took a deep breath and regaled the story of how Jack had figured out they were being watched, but they didn't know exactly who was watching them. How they had decided it was too dangerous and not to go chasing danger. Faiza mentioned the Post Office train incident with the dead body.

'Yes, we identified that as a hoax shortly afterwards and arrested two people who were in cahoots with Tim Plum. We tried so hard to find you and get you to safety. You should have listened to me.'

'We didn't know who to trust, Miss Corner – for all we knew you could have been one of the bad guys, like your Mr Plum,' said Wade defensively.

'He's not *my* Mr Plum, but point taken. Please continue.'

'Then he… well, he followed us somehow even though we were underground… how did he do that then?' asked Faiza.

Miss Corner looked at her notes and then at the three. 'He used a locational finding app common to most of us in CO8 – it can track anyone with a tracker, so I guess you had one planted on your person somewhere? The most common place is on clothing,' she said in a melancholy voice. 'The app is called *Kate Low*. His brother Plum used it so at some point he must have let Tim have it.'

Wade nodded and remembered he had dumped his jacket earlier at London Bridge station in favour of his less-than-stylish cowboy outfit.

Faiza spoke in more depth about getting to the disused office block and how they had to hide and run for their lives from who they now knew as Mr Tim.

'Interesting you should choose Embankment. It's the same area where Mr Tim's Grandad Plum was killed in the war. Kind of ironic.'

They nodded sagely and Wade smiled a smug smile as he heard the word *ironic* again. Wade munched a buttered scone as Faiza continued, 'So we got to Embankment with the idea of regrouping to come to you – honest – and stumbled across a shedload of gold!'

'*Stumbled across*?' Corner said scathingly. 'Highly unlikely knowing you lot, but we'll get the details later.'

'He threatened us with a taser, took the gold but his greed got the better of him – both he and the gold fell off the walkway…' Faiza's voice trailed off.

'With my rucksack,' added Jack crossly.

Miss Corner nodded and made a note. She peered over her glasses. 'Wow, it's been quite a day for you hasn't it?' she said understatedly. 'You've been through an amazing ordeal and even though it wasn't quite all of the gold, it's still an amazing find.'

'How much is still... out there?' asked Wade acting innocently.

'Too much and you are not, repeat not, to go looking for that either,' Miss Corner instructed.

'OK – what about Mr Tim or *Captain Grey* or Plum's brother or whatever he's called?' said Faiza in a burst of anger.

'We're still searching for Tim Plum and still have a team there, but we don't hold out much hope of finding him. Below that watery shaft are lots of side tunnels and feeder shafts, all of which are mostly inaccessible – they're flooded and very dangerous, and if he was weighed down with gold...'

None of them would admit it there, but they were not that unhappy to hear of his apparent demise. She sat back in her chair and peered over her glasses again. The atmosphere in the room cooled.

'Right, that's the niceties out of the way. Your statement that you had nothing to do with this isn't quite true is it, Miss Saab? I'm talking about the USB stick that you stole to try to get more information from. We have every right to be furious with you, again. You STOLE CO8 property – the USB stick – and jeopardised an ongoing investigation. I am not happy.' She peered over her glasses at the now sheepish three.

'It was a mystery and we just wanted to see what we could find out – you said it couldn't be found. It was a kind of challenge,' Wade said into the deafening silence.

'So, we'll have that USB stick back please, presumably you couldn't get into it either?' she asked.

All three shook their heads, consumed by making the lie as convincing as possible. She stared at them for a long time. Wade wondered if she could read their minds.

'No,' lied Faiza, cutting the scary silence, 'even *Billy Brainbox* here couldn't get into it.'

'Hmm,' said Miss Corner.

Wade tried to think of something to change the subject. 'Oh, oh!' he said, suddenly becoming very animated. 'You'll like this! When we spoke to *Captain Grey*, he told us that he got a journalist friend of his to tell lies and try to disrupt things.'

'Right, so we need to get hold of that journalist and have a discussion with him,' stated Corner.

'It's not a him, it's a her – it's *Bobbi Dudman*,' said Wade. 'Thought you'd like that!'

'Never liked her. Infuriating busybody.' Miss Corner beamed and signalled to Four-Five to do what needed to be done. The door hissed shut as he left.

Jack put his hand up. Miss Corner sighed and indicated for him to continue. 'I have a question. How long was Mr Ruby watching us for?' said Jack.

Corner nodded. 'That's a good question, Jack,' she said. 'Well I'm happy to say that someone who can answer that will be here momentarily.' They looked at her feeling puzzled, then turned to face the door, which opened with a swish. In front of them, now dressed in a suit, was their ex-temporary ICT teacher.

'Mr Ruby!' they said in unison.

He smiled back at them with a hand raised in greeting. 'Nice to see you again. Miss Saab, gentlemen.' Mr Ruby came and sat next to Miss Corner.

'Yes, when we found out there may be a possible threat to yourselves, we put an agent in place – I believe you already know Agent Six-Four?' Miss Corner said.

'Good disguise, Mr Ruby,' said Wade. 'We thought you were—'

'An annoyingly nosy supply teacher with a disarming smile? I had to get you into my confidence somehow. Had to try and ensure you were safe. I've been following you for some time now. It's me that followed you to the Monument and let CO8 know you'd found something. We even hacked your computer. After some time, we could see someone was following *you*, so I kept tabs on them too.'

'I was almost there, I *almost* got it. I knew there was something amiss – some of the things you were saying!' complained Jack.

'You show promise, you three. And yes, you did see me at Stockwell and a few other places too – I was on your tail. Had to ensure your safety.' He shrugged his shoulders. 'Sorry we lost track of you after you were at London Bridge, but we caught Tim Plum on CCTV at Embankment so I hotfooted it there.'

'We knew how sneaky and resourceful ex-agent Plum was and after the publicity from the first hoard you found, we sent in Agent Six-Four to keep an eye on you,' added Miss Corner.

'Indeed. Good news is that we retrieved your rucksack, Jack, but we'll be keeping that for a while as it's got lots of gold in it at the moment,' said Mr Ruby happily. 'Oh, but I do have something for you.' Mr Ruby fished in his pocket and pulled out something wrapped in a plastic bag. He handed it to Jack who looked inside. 'We found it on the lower walkway – think it belongs to you.'

'My Spitfire!' Jack stared at it beaming, as he turned the battered model Spitfire in his hands.

'So, you'll shortly be heading home and that's when the real music will be faced I expect,' said Corner. The faces of the three showed real fear. 'In the meantime I'll need more details on exactly what happened, then I have to go to see one of our old *friends* and tell him the bad news about his brother.'

'Wish I could be there,' said Faiza determinedly.

'I'll pass on your best wishes.' Miss Corner sat back in her chair and nodded. 'I'll be expecting you to give signed depositions over the next few days with as much detail as you can remember, leave nothing out. But, for now, it's almost home time.' She smiled, then leaned forward conspiratorially.

'Despite your mistakes and sometimes brazen escapades, you've all done amazing things in exceedingly difficult circumstances. You found the gold. Again! There has been talk of an award.'

'Ooh, what award?' asked Wade keenly.

Miss Corner looked left and right and motioned for them to move in even closer. 'It's rumoured that it could be the King's Gallantry medal but keep that under your hat.' She shuffled her papers again as the three looked on speechless.

'Is that a *gold* medal?' Wade asked nonchalantly.

37

Miss Corner sat opposite the dejected-looking manacled man opposite her.

'And so that's that. We're still looking for him or his body.' She was sorry to have to deliver bad news, but this was tempered by the Plum family bringing it on themselves.

'If you had just come to us, we could have saved all this including the... unfortunateness.'

'You did this. They did this,' he said quietly, looking into her eyes. The assured confidence had faded.

'What we did, what *they* did, was this: they defeated you, they avoided your revengeful plan and, yes, they led me and CO8 a right merry dance at times,' she replied.

He humphed and looked away.

'But I would take them over you any day. They have more spirit, more gumption, more loyalty and more brains in their little fingers than you ever had. And now you and your brother have paid the price of greed. I feel pity for you.'

'Don't feel pity for me, you preachy old hag,' he spluttered.

'You really are regressing aren't you? I'll take that as my cue to leave.' She stood up and moved towards the door.

'I've got a lot of time coming up, Miss Corner, and I'm going to spend it—' shouted Plum.

Corner moved over to him and held a finger up in front of his face. He went quiet.

'You will have a lot of time, it's true. But you're going to be spending all of it just mulling over how you, *you*, could have stopped all of this from happening. I hope you've learned now that the gold was nothing but a curse for you. I know I seem to keep on saying it but really – Goodbye, Mr Plum.' She exited the room followed by a smiling Agent Six-Four.

Plum, *Mr Blue*, just sat staring furiously but helplessly at the door, a man who had lost everything.

'Call for you, Miss Corner,' came the tinny voice of Miss Place over the car's intercom ten minutes later as they headed back to LPS House. She put down her paper and peered over her glasses.

'Ugh, really – can't I find any peace? Is it important?'

'It's Agent Three-Seven, ma'am – he's at Embankment Station and says it's urgent.'

Miss Corner indicated to have the call routed through to her and then listened intently.

Faiza, Wade and Jack lounged in the back of the large blacked-out limousine as they headed over Tower Bridge.

'This is becoming a habit,' said Wade waving at people for no particular reason.

'I could get used to it too,' added Jack. He admired the plush surroundings and plumped up one of the large cushions before sitting back smiling.

'Wonder if they'll find Mr Tim,' said Wade to no-one.

'With any luck he's gone for good... else he'll have me to deal with,' Faiza said firmly.

'Listen, I'm glad you're ok,' said Wade quietly, turning to Faiza.

'Not as much as me,' replied Faiza. 'Thanks for... well you know.' She turned to look at Jack and added, 'Hey, we make a good team eh?'

'You know what, we do,' said Jack and they all made an air clap. 'I'm kind of glad that it's all over now though.'

They laughed.

'Good team or not, let's agree never to do this again,' said Faiza.

'Agreed,' said Jack smiling right at her.

Wade pondered for a second. 'Well, I was wondering where the rest of the gold is buried – there are loads of unexplored tunnels,' he said with a twinkle in his eye.

'Oh I expect there are loads of mysteries and hidden hoards down there... just waiting to be discovered,' muttered Jack. 'After all we only found about seventy bars, so somewhere there are fifty bars just waiting...' His voice trailed off.

'I like the idea of tracking people... what was that app? *Kate Low*?' said Wade excitedly.

'I think we should use that as a callsign if we're in trouble again,' said Jack seriously.

'Not going to happen, is it? Because it's all *over* now and we're not doing it again,' insisted Faiza firmly. 'Whether there's fifty bars left or not.'

Wade looked at Jack and then at Faiza, with a wry smile. 'Well... when it all dies down and it's a lot safer, maybe we'll just go and look at places on the Underground again, eh? Just a look of course,' he said with fake disdain.

The other two looked at each other and made a thoughtful face.

'Maybe, when it's all faded a bit,' said Jack, quietly liking the idea. 'We never did find out who the woman in the old black and white picture was, so there are still lots of unanswered questions…'

'*For now,* we'll agree we're never doing that again,' she replied and the other two nodded. 'Hey, you can explain to my dad what happened – tell him we had to rescue you or something.'

'Only if you tell my mum that it wasn't our fault!'

'My dad will be a bit worried, but my great-grandad will be ecstatic, and I'll be able to tell stories about this for years!' exclaimed Jack.

'I hope you're going to tell him how it was me that saved us from a madman and how I got us out of there by my genius thinking. If it hadn't been for my—' But the rest of Wade's speech was cut short by the sound of him being battered with cushions.

Epilogue

The old woman sighed as she headed towards the front door. Her little dog yapped as he came running in from the drawing room.

'Leave it alone, *Oro Fluffikins!*' she said as she reached down to pick up the paper from the doormat and scanned the front page. *Goldbusters Strike Again*, it screamed. She smiled and sat in her armchair.

'I'm sure I've seen that young man somewhere before, what do you think, my lovely *Oro*?' She showed it to her dog, who yapped and ran around in circles. The picture on the front was of Faiza, Wade and Jack smiling next to the Monument.

She read part of the newspaper and her smile turned to a frown.

'Oh my, oh my, it can't be. That's our... that's my—' She was looking at two pictures further down the piece. One of them was of a frowning man in a Hi-Viz vest and under it was the name, *Mr Tim Plum*. Next to it was a grey picture of Horatio Plum and a young woman taken during the war. She screwed her eyes up and ran her finger over Plum's features.

'Gosh he was so young then, so clever and young... and so was she,' she mumbled.